T0182490

BLUE
～
DANUBE

An imprint of Blue Guides Limited, a Somerset Books company
Unit 2, Old Brewery Road, Wiveliscombe, Somerset TA4 2PW

Distributed in the USA by WW Norton & Company, Inc.
500 Fifth Avenue, New York, NY 10110.

Translated from the Hungarian: *A zenélő angyal* (1933)
English translation © Annabel Barber 2024

ISBN 978-1-916568-04-4

Cover: Detail from Giovanni Bellini's *Madonna and Saints* (1488)
in the church of the Frari, Venice. Photo © Blue Guides.

Every effort has been made to contact the copyright owners
of material reproduced in this book.
We would be pleased to hear from any copyright owners
we have been unable to reach.

Printed and bound in Great Britain by TJ Books.

 somersetbooks.com/bluedanube

VENETIAN ANGEL

Ferenc Molnár

Translated by Annabel Barber

BLUE DANUBE

Foreword

Ferenc Molnár, my grandfather, had to leave Hungary in 1937 because of the Fascist tide there. He aimed to take refuge in America, but his first stop on the way to New York was Venice, a city he loved dearly. In this novel he calls it 'a wonder of the world'.

Daily life in Budapest was still undisturbed in 1933. Molnár was seen daily in his straw hat, sparkling monocle in the right eye, strolling along the Duna Corso, the promenade on the Pest side of the Danube, stretching from the Elisabeth Bridge to the Chain Bridge. Already a well-known dramatist and writer in Europe and America, he was greeted at every step, even by friendly strangers. The Athenaeum publishing house asked him for a new novel. What should he write about? He submitted a manuscript without much of a story, its title inspired by a little flute-blowing putto at the bottom of Bellini's *Madonna* in the Frari church in Venice. In essence, the story is a love triangle, a romance coloured with intrigue and jealousy. Molnár, with the skill of a psychologist, describes a young woman on the verge of becoming a grown-up, still unversed in the complications of adult life, still a dreamer. The action is played out against the backdrop of the Venice which Molnár knew so well, with its fascinating history and its narrow little alleyways. He maintains that living abroad makes one different. Does it? Perhaps less so today than it did in Molnár's time. Now the world's populace is becoming a global melting pot of nationalities and races. But the main theme remains eternal. The protagonists come into sharp focus in Molnár's mirror. A mirror which is able to show not only virtues, but every human foible and frailty.

Mátyás Sárközi
Hampstead, 2024

1

The waterfront façade of the Doge's Palace glowed pink in the June sunshine. In the midday heat, the normally bustling quaysides of the Molo and Riva degli Schiavoni were all but deserted. The straw hat vendors and the glass bead sellers had retreated to doze in small patches of shade. Beneath the high stone quay, the gondolas lay sleeping side by side between their crooked wooden mooring posts. The quiet of the summer lunch hour had descended and in secluded corners all over the city, hidden away from the heat and the glare, people were sitting down to their midday meals. The streets were empty.

Beneath the waterfront arcade of the Doge's Palace, which at this hour was in deep shadow and where only a slight breeze stirred, a man and woman appeared, walking towards St Mark's Square. Their steps kept time, brisk, like a soldier's march. The woman's heels echoed loudly on the wide stone flags. They were talking Hungarian. One word floated out:

'Attila?'

They smiled. They were young. The girl looked about twenty. She was slender and seemed more animated than her companion. A small, dark blue hat was clamped over her mane of thick fair hair. Her smiling eyes were restless and irregular. There was a charming, ever-so-slight unevenness about their gaze. She was a supple, fresh, straightforward sort of girl, dressed in a dark blue skirt and a dark blue, short-sleeved blouse. There was nothing remotely matronly about her. She had a slightly turned-up nose. A light scarf striped in rainbow colours drifted around her bare, sun-browned arms. The way she walked along beside her companion, determinedly keeping pace with him, the way she talked and smiled, then looked at him and laughed; the way she fluttered her coloured scarf—all these things seemed to suggest a certain hyperactivity. Her companion, by contrast, was calm and placid. His dark hair was receding a little— ever such a little. His expression was impassive, perhaps even stern, but when he smiled a look of true benevolence suffused his face. He was not the raffish, debonair kind of man that women usually find so appealing.

The girl laughed. 'You're saying this is all because of Attila the Hun?'

'Absolutely.'

'So we Hungarians had a hand in the founding of this place.'

'If one can call it founding.'

'Well yes, I think one can,' she said. 'It's a kind of founding, after all.' She stopped walking and gravely began to explain herself. 'You told me that the Venetians fled from Attila to the smaller islands. Which means that Venice as we know it, this wonder of the world, wouldn't exist if Attila hadn't chased those poor people into the sea.'

'That's true.'

'So without Attila there would be no Venice.'

'No.'

'You see?'

She laughed up at him, a tinkling, girlish, brittle sort of laugh. They resumed walking, then stopped on the corner to look up at the Campanile. The man was clearly taking the girl on a tour of the sights. They looked up at the bell-tower and then the girl looked into her companion's eyes, concentrating hard on what he was saying. From time to time she glanced up again, at the great brick tower rearing into the sky, then back at her companion, a slight frown showing how deeply she was paying attention.

The young man had got to know Venice fairly well in the two years he had been living there. He had begun by earnestly studying its history. Then he had started taking Hungarian visitors on guided tours. That is not always a very pleasant task. Very often the 'guidees' are not content to submit to the other person's authority. They keep trying to assert themselves, saying things like, 'Oh, I know all this from photographs,' or 'Oh, it's exactly how I expected it to be.' This young girl was nothing like that. She was so keen, so obligingly admiring, such a vision of youth and good breeding. She was a pleasure to take around. This was the second day the young man had spent with her, quietly and succinctly explaining the city. He had very little time for it since he worked in a bank most of the day and could only find time during his lunch hour or after he clocked off in the afternoon. The girl had arrived in Venice with her parents two days previously. This was her first visit.

'I expect all the Budapest people are awfully tiresome,' she said. 'Father tells me you're a sort of acting ambassador here. You have to organise rooms for everyone. I can just imagine how trying you must find it.'

'I've got used to it. Two years is a long time.'

'We pestered you about a room too, didn't we?'

'No, no, please, it was a pleasure. I hope the hotel is to your liking?'

'Oh yes.'

'Your father is satisfied with the accommodation, I trust? He can be hard to please.'

'Oh, I know! He's never happy with things the way they are.' The girl smiled into the middle distance, her words warm and indulgently forgiving of the father she clearly adored. 'I mean—well, you know him, after all.'

It was true. Before the young man had come to Italy, he had spent two years as secretary to the girl's father.

The girl looked out at the lagoon and heaved a small sigh.

'I envy you. It must be so lovely to live here.'

Across the water, wedged between military barracks, the church of San Giorgio Maggiore glowed pink on its island.

It was as if its walls had obtained their colour from centuries of sunbathing. A deep terracotta, like the forearms of the old fishermen and the gondoliers. The church's brick bell-tower was tipped with green. A little further to the right, on top of the squat tower of the Dogana, sat a golden globe, gleaming in the sunshine. The Venetian lagoon, that flat, far-stretching, waveless impostor of a sea, was a bright, bright blue. The shades of blue one encounters in the Latin Mediterranean are not in the least afraid of the German word *kitsch*; they dare to be as blue as the mood takes them.

The pair set off across St Mark's Square. Once again the girl heaved a little sigh.

'It must be pure peaches and cream being able to live here!'

'It is. Peaches and cream, indeed. I sometimes feel like a child who has been so good he's force-fed treats from morning till night.'

'Aren't you happy here?'

'It's not easy to be happy on one's own.'

'I know.'

The girl breathed the words with a sad little smile, her head on one side, looking at the young man quizzically.

With the calm that came so naturally to him, without the least hint of superiority or sarcasm, he said,

'You should get married.'

The girl just looked at him. 'Oh, come now! Aren't you ashamed of yourself, talking like that to a young girl? A man of your age? How old are you, anyway?'

'Thirty.'

The girl let out a low whistle, her face grave. The man stopped walking.

'Does that seem a lot?'

'I'll say!'

They resumed their wandering, under the arcades. The shop windows were full of colourful books and albums, all with rich gilded bindings. There were hand-made goblets, too, scarlet and emerald green with gold bases and gold stems—there was gold everywhere. There were colour photographs in golden frames. And heaps of glass beads, glass flowers, brass gondolas, lamps. The arcades in front of Caffè Florian were hung with huge crimson awnings against the sun. The girl walked quickly past the window displays. Gold, gold—everything, but *everything* made of gold! It had started in the sixteenth century. Venetian artisans had begun smothering everything in gold. Not just iron and marble or silk and glass; the gilding extended to the very ropes they used to tie up their ships, the oars they used to steer them with. They even gilded their savoury pâtés and their sugary cakes—even the bread they baked had gold dust in it. And the Venetian artisan is still in love with gold. There is gold in the mosaics, gold in the glass beads, gold in every stick of furniture, in the iron railings, the drinking glasses, wallpapers, book bindings, wallets, slippers—there is even gold in the names of the lowliest hotels: Stella d'Oro, Leone d'Oro, the 'Golden Star', the 'Golden Lion'... Even fountain pens—which are jet black everywhere else, like the gondolas are in Venice—even the fountain pens wink golden in the shop windows of the *Serenenissima*.

The young man was beginning to get restless. Reflected in the glass shopfront, the girl caught him looking at his watch. Slyly she attempted to extract a compliment.

'I expect it's a bore, my making you drag me around like this. You'll come to hate me.'

'Perhaps I will,' came the answer. 'One can never know. But it certainly won't be because of that.'

'It's all Father's fault, you know. He promised that you would be my guide. Mother is still very unwell, she hardly leaves her room, and Father has to travel such a great deal. Venice is just his base camp, you see. He's got meetings in Trieste, in Milan, in Rome. So here I am with you and I'm afraid you've got to lump it.'

She waited for him to protest but all she got was a polite and tolerant smile. She plunged on hurriedly, putting the minor little slight behind her, moving the conversation forward.

'But please let's not spend our time endlessly looking at paintings. And don't give me any lectures me about architecture, either. Instead I want you to tell me about real life. For example this fishy smell. What is it?'

She stopped, her delicate little nose sniffing the air.

'It's not a fishy smell,' the young man told her. 'It's the

smell of water.'

'Seriously? Have I been rude to Venice by suggesting it was fish?'

'Well yes, I rather think you have.'

She turned round to face St Mark's, clicked her heels together and bowed.

'Venice, I crave your forgiveness!'

Then she walked quickly under the colonnade, out of the square and on towards San Moisè. Her companion found himself somewhat left behind.

'Don't be in such a rush!'

The girl waved her brightly striped scarf in a sweeping, all-encompassing gesture. 'But I want to see all of this, and *understand* it, as it is now, today. I don't want a load of old history and I don't need any of that Italian language stuff. I can never remember a single word in any case. I want the here and now, all of it. I certainly don't want names and dates. You've been so kind to me, so patient, but the way you're looking at me now—well, I think you must find me a bit ridiculous.'

'Ridiculous?'

She raced on, leaving him behind again. When he finally caught up with her, she stopped.

'Do you realise that it's exactly two years since I last saw you?'

'I haven't got any younger.'

'Neither have I.'

'How old are you? Nineteen?'

'Good heavens no! I'm twenty.'

'You are or you're about to be?'

'I am.'

An elderly newspaper vendor was standing next to them. '*Carlinoberlino!*' he called out. Then he went on his way.

The girl laughed. 'What did he say?'

'*Carlino, Berlino.* He's selling two papers. The *Resto del Carlino* and the *Berliner Tagesblatt.*'

'And he's turned them into...*Carlinoberlino!*'

'I say, you did that awfully well.'

'Did I?'

At last! she thought. A bit of recognition. She looked down the long narrow street, between the high houses, towards the water. These aren't really streets, she thought, they're just deep fissures between brown, five-storey blocks. At the far end, the water shone dazzlingly bright, and there was that golden globe again, on top of the Dogana. The girl called out down the long, empty, cavernous street, calling out to the water, to the golden-topped tower:

'*Carlinoberlino!*' She laughed up at her companion. 'Well, how else do you expect me to behave? The Germans have a word for it: *Übermut.* I suppose we'd say over-excitement. Well I admit it, I'm happy. Ooh—there's that lagoon smell again!'

'No,' he said. 'This time it's the *rio* you can smell. That's what they call a small canal, here, a *rio.*'

They climbed the wide steps of the stone bridge. Under its arch was a clutch of gondolas, nestled together in the grey-green lymph of the canal. The young man and the girl looked up at the façade of San Moisè, smoke-smirched and thickly encrusted with statuary, 'the frightful façade,' as John Ruskin disgustedly expressed it, 'illustrative of the last degradation of the Renaissance.' And as they stood there, the white-blazered gondoliers called out to them from the water, offering their services with eager abandon, as if bidding at auction.

'D'you fancy it?' the young man asked, pointing at the gondolas.

'Not now, thank you. I went with Father yesterday, in the afternoon, after you'd gone. He took me all over the place, up and down the little canals. Father knows this city so well. We'll do it together some other time. Not now. Let's go back.'

'Where?'

'To the Piazza, to sit outside a café in the sun. My word, how uneven these steps are!'

She clutched at his arm as they picked their way back down from the bridge. She glanced out at the water again, back down the dark alley. There were ships out there now. And once again, that golden globe. She let go of his arm.

'Isn't it divine!'

'I'm glad you like it.'

'You're sweet. You sounded so pleased, as if Venice was really your city. Did you buy that shirt here?'

'Yes. Why?'

'I like the colour. True navy blue. Is it silk?'

'No.'

She reached out and tested the shirt fabric between her thumb and forefinger.

'Isn't it too warm?'

'No.'

'Dark blue doesn't really go with blue eyes, you know. White would be better.' She looked him in the eye, smiling happily. 'You can't believe your ears, can you? Fancy me having nothing better to worry about! Well I have, of course. It's just that this city is making me giddy. It's a shame one can't roar around it in a motor car. Do you know why Mother was so glad to be coming to Venice? Because for once we'd be somewhere where I wouldn't be able to drive. I had an accident last year. I think the town of Szentendre[1] must have the twistiest-twiniest streets of anywhere in the world. Should you ever happen to go there, be sure to drive extremely slowly. I crashed into a brick lorry. It was his fault. That's where I got this.'

She showed him her scar, pointing her little finger at her shoulder. Her shoulders were suntanned, slightly boyish, like the shoulders of a classical terracotta statue. Her slim, well-formed arm curved upwards in a gentle arc. She showed him this token of her accident almost proudly, fixing him with her uneven gaze. Their eyes met and held and she smiled shyly. She had forgotten to drop her arm back down by her side. The young man stared at her shapely young shoulder.

'Where did you get so brown?'

She dropped her arm at last. They continued on their way.

'In Tahifalu[2], by the Danube. It's so beautiful there, lying in a boat as it swings on its moorings, with a damp flannel across my forehead, rubbing myself with oil that I get from the fishermen. Oh, I can just lie there roasting for hours, dozing in the noonday calm... The only thing that breaks the silence is the geese, swimming across the water in great flocks—across and then back again. And then silence, silence... And now and again, from the further bank, comes the creak of a passing cart...'

Across the Piazzetta, beyond the Molo, she looked out at the open water. But what she saw, in her mind's eye, was the Danube.

'You love the Danube,' the young man said softly.

'Oh I do! The dear old, scruffy old Hungarian Danube! The waterline all deep, damp silt, with sharp brown shells sticking out of it. And further up the bank, huge pebbles with bits of broken pottery jumbled up among them. And tufts of dry, parched grass... A rusty tin which has lain there since it was discarded three years ago... And the scrubby little bushes, now out of the water, now submerged again for days on end...' She paused. 'Are those battleships?'

'Yes.'

'Italian?'

'No. British.'

'Can you see the flags from here?'

'Of course I can.'

She screwed up her eyes.

'I can't.'

They went back to the Piazza, towards the serried ranks of little café tables, all made of iron. St Mark's Square is the world's biggest cast-iron furniture mart.

The Piazza had filled up. British sailors, dressed from head to toe in white, were sauntering up and down in twos and fours, among the pigeons. Germans. Gaggles of children. Their piercing shrieks and the sounds of all the hundreds of other conversations filled the Piazza with a kind of soft hum. Here, in this fortune-blessed city, which for a thousand years has never seen a horse, a carriage, a car, a bicycle—hardly even a nanny-powered perambulator—here the human voice is restored to its rightful place. No automobile or tram can drown it out. In the quiet of the evening, the sound of human footsteps can clearly be heard—that is, if the café musicians are not playing too loud. A platoon of British sailors went by, armed with rifles. Photographers. More Germans. A scattering of Hungarians, enjoying an evening promenade. Voices: '*Abendbrot in der Taverna*', or 'Piri, don't keep running off ahead like that, how many times do I have to tell you?' But the people who made the most noise were the pigeon-food vendors. Standing at their little booths, they out-rattled each other with their tins of dried corn, vying with each other to attract as many pigeons and would-be pigeon feeders as they could. The pigeon-food vendors of St Mark's are the world's smallest-scale grain traders.

'If I didn't think it was silly, I'd buy some barley for the pigeons,' the girl said.

'They don't feed them barley.'

'What, then?'

'Sweetcorn and split peas.'

'Are they tame?'

'Tame? They're bold as brass,' the young man told her, glaring at them with loathing, as only someone who lives in Venice can.

'Let's sit here.'

They sat down on two iron chairs. They both winced. The chairs were scorching hot from the sun. Neither of them wanted to be the one to stand up again. They both sat there on the searing metal, staring at each other. Then they burst out laughing.

'It's like György Dózsa[3]!' the girl exclaimed. She reached out to touch the metal tabletop. That was boiling hot as well. She looked about her. Not many people had chosen to sit in that particular spot.

'Is this the famous Caffè Florian?'

'No. It's the Lavena. Why don't you sit there, facing the Basilica?'

The girl did as he suggested. She screwed up her eyes to

look at the façade, which was on fire from the sun.

'Divine! It's not a very tall building, though. Interesting—such a famous church and yet it's really quite low-slung.'

The sun shone on the façade, selectively, like a theatre spotlight picking out certain parts of the stage. What it revealed was a gold, grey and pink forest of squat columns, cupola-topped and statue-and-relief-encrusted, under a bright blue sky. The gilded mosaics of saints and martyrs were bathed in sunlight. And above them, majestically tinctured with pale gold, standing out against an azure ground, bursting from a firmament of fist-sized golden stars, was the great winged Lion, like an elaborately illuminated fairytale beast, its front paw resting on the golden gospel. From out of a froth of lacy masonry, spiky turrets shot into the sky, each one tipped with a gleaming golden weathervane. And in amongst them, golden-winged angels bearing golden thuribles climbed upwards and upwards, all the way up to the mighty twenty-branched cross that surmounts each of the five domes. And there at the summit, on five times twenty golden arms, five times twenty golden orbs were sparkling in the rays of the sun.

Above the domes, high in the sky, a single cloud floated. It was the only one. It looked like one of those bright white pillowy meerschaum excrescences that used to be a feature of tobacconists' window displays. It was not in the least like an ordinary cloud. There was nothing wispy about it, it did not look like candy floss, or smoke, or a gossamer veil. Quite the contrary, it was hard and solid and stiff, as if carved in relief, pinned rigidly against the backdrop of the blue June sky and blinding in its whiteness. And the sky, it must be said, had something of the same quality. It had no notion of gradation or tint or shade; there were no hints of grey or of pale green or pink. It was purest, unadulterated blue. Unambiguously blue, like an upholsterer's swatch. And against this blue, silhouetted in front of it, were the angels, teetering on top of every pediment. The wings they held aloft were of the very purest gold, and the sky was the very purest azure, the purest that has existed since time immemorial.

A waiter appeared. Somehow it seems to be a universal law. Wherever a view is the most enchanting, along comes a waiter and places himself slap in front of it.

'*Cosa prendono?*'

'What shall we have?' the girl asked.

The decided way in which the young man resolved her dilemma was somewhat overdone, she felt.

'At this time of day, *mazagran*. *Caffè in ghiaccio*.'

The waiter retreated. The golden angels were free to glisten once more against the bluest-blue of the sky. Still looking at them, her eyes narrowed, the girl asked quietly,

'What's *mazagran*?'

'Black coffee. With lots of ice.'

Still without taking her eyes off the golden angels, she said, 'I've just learned something new. D'you know, I only enjoy learning things from men. It was from a man that I learned, just a week ago in Cortina, that the Dolomites are named after a French geologist called Dolomieux. One never learns that sort of thing from a woman.'

'Who was he, this man in Cortina?'

'That would be telling.'

She still had not taken her eyes off the angels on the Basilica roof. For some time she just looked at them, saying nothing. Then finally her eyes came down to earth, to the table, to the young man's hand.

'Have you always had that ring?'

'Always.'

'I don't remember it. Don't take your hand away.'

She stared at the ring. It was a signet ring. A ring with a plain blue stone. A plain blue stone on the young man's brown hand.

'It was my grandfather's,' he told her. 'Who was the man in Cortina?'

But the girl just responded with a question of her own.

'Do you work terribly hard?'

'No. Just at the bank.' He pointed behind him, under the arcades. 'It's down there. I'm in the credit department because I speak German. The Germans have always loved Venice. The Germans and the Hungarians. It's a good department to work in. One gets to deal with a better class of customer…'

'Women? Rich American ladies?'

'Oh, plenty of those.'

'Beautiful women?'

'Yes, sometimes. Extremely so. I'm pretty well set up here, I have to admit. I live in a small *pensione* but it's perfectly decent. I'm grateful to your father. If he hadn't helped with the bank—you know, with all his contacts...'

'Then what?'

'Then—well, I must say, I don't know. There was nothing for me at home. When your father was an MP, he needed a secretary but now—well, Miss Rosenfeld can take care of everything. Good Heavens, Miss Rosenfeld! How is she?'

'Uglier than ever, thank you for asking. She's on holiday at the moment, summering at our place. She'll be swimming in the Danube, I expect. In her spectacles.'

'If I'd stayed at home I'd have hit rock bottom, there are no two ways about it. But here I'm making a pretty good fist of things. Not to say that I'm one of life's prizewinners or anything, but I'm doing all right. And I have every Saturday afternoon off—and all day Sunday...'

He fell silent, waiting as the waiter set the two glasses of *mazagran* on the table. The girl rather liked the sound of what he said, the modesty with which he said it. Not that any of it was particularly interesting; it was just genuine conversation.

'I wouldn't say you look *happy*, precisely,' she said. 'But contented, at least.'

'That's a fair assessment.'

The young man did indeed appear contented as he stirred his coffee and looked out at the Piazza. He had the perfect secretary's manner. His expression, untroubled by any particular emotion, was that of the perfect courteous clerk, an expression to win a client's trust. The kind of expression that responds to an anxious summons with a 'Don't let it worry you, Madam' or an 'I'll speak to His Excellency immediately, Sir.' Restrained and yet intensely reassuring, giving the fretting customer the feeling that they have placed their affairs in capable hands, that the problem has half gone away already.

The young man took a sip of his coffee and went on, 'So yes, it's fair to say that I'm contented. Contentment comes from having nothing and no one to fear. And I haven't.'

She could well believe him.

They drank their coffee, looking out at the water. The Molo was crowded with people, with big groups making their way to the Basilica, children with their tutors and governesses. It was filled with noise. Ships were sounding their horns, little launches were tooting their klaxons. And across the water rose the red-brick tower of San Giorgio, with a ship in front of it, its myriad coloured flags a-flutter. The water was alight with golden reflections—blue and gold, blue and white, blue-white-gold in every direction.

The young man was saying something, speaking quietly, but the girl wasn't listening to him. When he finished, all she said was,

'Your voice has got deeper.'

'I don't think it has. It must be because you haven't heard it for so long.'

'I envy you,' she said again. 'You've found a way of breaking out into the world. Whereas I just feel weighed down by worry. My family is falling apart. Mother was in the sanatorium for months; Father is perpetually away, doing his business deals. "Good Christian that I am, I've adopted a Jewish profession." That's the way he likes to put it. We're an unsettled lot. Which is why it feels so good being with you. Back at home—I mean, my goodness, all those silly fops! It drives me absolutely mad! It's not their manners that I mind, it's their *attitude*. Count Micky, Count Bobby. Castles and cocktails, bridge and tango, rumba and money worries. They can discuss the head waiter of a café as if he was a figure of international importance. Analysing his character, praising or criticising—as if he were a cabinet minster. They go on and on and on. I mean, I know so much about Teddy, the waiter from the Kit-Kat Bar, that he might as well be my uncle! And yet I've never clapped eyes on him, nor the Kit-Kat Bar either for that matter. Poor specimens of manhood, all of them, believe me. I say—you've got a moustache. I've only just noticed.'

She wasn't being entirely truthful. She checked herself. She sensed that she was being insincere, too skittish. She was overdoing it. She patted her face with her hand.

'Are your cheeks burning?'

'Yes.'

'That'll be from the sun.'

'Quite likely.' She cast him an appraising look.

He seemed embarrassed. 'What are you staring at?' he wanted to know.

'At what you're wearing. At the way it says "foreigner". It's not something one can put one's finger on but it's there all the same. It only happens with men, though. Women are far more international. Wherever we end up, we always manage to blend in. But men… The trademark Budapest double-breasted overcoat, the dark blue twill suit—oh, you can tell a Hungarian man a mile off! No one else wears that sort of thing. Well yes, the overcoat perhaps, but anyone else's trousers would be grey or white, not *blue*. And another thing that marks you out as Hungarian is the lack of precious metal. Your watch is made of steel. So is your matchbox holder. You carry your cigarettes in a paper packet. I'll bet you haven't a gold pencil.'

'No.'

'And your handkerchiefs are plain white. That's such a fine, decent Hungarian habit. Do you know where the best gentlemen's tailors are?'

'In London.'

'No. In Madrid. I learned that from the man who told me about the Dolomites.'

'And you still won't tell me who he was?'

'No.'

The young man smiled. 'Have you done much travelling?'

'Only since last year. That's when I was launched into the world. We went to Kitzbühel in the winter. So I've been to Switzerland. And after that to Paris. And Cannes in the spring.'

Slowly, methodically, she began shredding the drinking straw that had come with her coffee. First she tore it lengthways, then crumbled it into little pieces. Soon there was a little pile of chaff on the table in front of her, which she began pushing about with her finger. The young man paid. He handed over a note, was given his change in coins. As she arranged and rearranged the little bits of broken straw, the girl collected her thoughts.

I'm nervous, she told herself. I'm blabbering. I've let myself get carried away by the mad, noisy, sun-drenched, blue-and-gold, lagoon-scented air. This improbable place is intoxicating me. Or am I just play-acting? Overdoing the part of giddy young girl? As for him, he is almost comical with that grave secretarial manner of his. The way he orders the drinks, the way he pays the bill. I don't like the idea of costing him money. The poor fellow probably has everything worked out to the very last *lira*. And the coffee here is expensive. Probably because of all that ice...

By the time they left the café, she had whittled all this down to a single idea.

'You were born to be a secretary. Don't you think?'

'Heavens, how grand that makes me feel!'

28

Once more they were keeping time as they walked along, as if on a drill, making their way from the Piazza to the waterfront. The girl continued.

'My father's secretary… Good gracious, how I looked up to you two or three years ago! You had a briefcase. You had a jacket. You were better looking in those days.' She cast him a sideways glance. 'Your hair is receding.'

The young man did not look at her in return. He continued staring straight ahead.

'You certainly aren't letting me down lightly,' he said good-humouredly.

They walked on in silence for a bit. Then she said,

'That time in Tahifalu…do you remember?'

She stopped. She was smiling. Her companion mechanically walked on a little way, then turned.

'Remember what?'

'That evening when everyone was drinking wine in the garden… When you carried me down to the Danube.'

She said it on a smile, but her voice was bashful.

'Of course,' the young man replied. His voice was soothing and pleasant. 'Of course I remember.'

Down by the water, once again, the girl looked out at the golden globe on the Dogana di Mare. And once again at the blue and grey British battleships. Then she turned and looked up at the two tall granite columns reaching high into the sky.

'One of them has the winged lion on it. I know what that

is, it's Venice's symbol. But who's that on the other one?'

'A saint. St Theodore. He was patron of the city before St Mark.'

'But not any longer?'

'No.'

'Come on.' She made to walk between the columns.

The young man seized her bare hand, warm with the afternoon sun. 'You mustn't.'

'Mustn't what?'

'Go between the columns like that.'

'Whyever not? I mean, *those* people...' She pointed to all the people who were wandering in and out between the columns.

'They don't know about the old superstition. This used to be a place of execution. There was a gallows between the columns. It's bad luck to walk between them. A proud and haughty Doge once thumbed his nose at the superstition by landing here and leading his entire glittering retinue between the columns. Not long afterwards he had his head chopped off, despite his seventy-seven years.'

'Interesting,' the girl said, then calmly walked between the columns. She called to the young man. 'Come on, I dare you!'

He hesitated for an instant, then shook his head with a nervous smile.

'No.'

He walked round the columns, rejoining the girl on the

other side. She stood waiting for him, shaking her head. Then they continued walking, in silence, back under the arcades, the way they had come. The girl kept her eyes fixed on the ground, a little abstracted. Then, on a tentative little smile, she said,

'Did you know that in Cannes, a Hamilton asked me to marry him?'

2

The evening which the girl had described, with somewhat forced insouciance, as 'that evening when everyone was drinking wine in the garden' had happened at the family's summer house in Tahifalu, about two years previously. There had been a dinner party for a few friends and neighbours, people who also had land and summer villas on the Danube. The Lietzen house—which the girl's father would not allow anyone to call a villa—was a long way from the village, on a gentle slope with views out across the river. It had originally been built as a bungalow by a modest civil servant, a man in the excise office. Mr Lietzen had bought it for a song from his widow, had altered it, enlarged it, added an upper floor and extended the Danube-facing terrace at the front. He had not spent quite as much on it as Louis XIV did on Versailles but nevertheless, he enjoyed making the comparison. The final result was a large, expansive summer house, of the kind that well-to-do Hungarians like to own. Its vast gardens sloped down to the river, separated by iron railings from the orchard and vegetable beds, which both stretched all the way to the main road along the waterfront. Above and behind the house, where the land rose steeply, a small vineyard straggled up the sunny slope, devouring the wages of the hired hands who attacked it with hoes and pruning shears, greedily gobbling copper sulphate and—in years when there wasn't a frost—yielding parsimonious amounts of extremely sour wine. When this happened, the cost of harvesting the grapes came to more than the value of the land. Stephen Lietzen decided to punish his vineyard by bringing all wine production to a summary halt. If the vines produced any half-decent grapes, the family would eat them. If they didn't, then table grapes purchased from Nándor Horváth[4] would be brought down from Budapest. Production on the rest of the 'estate' was managed in much the same way. The main point of it was that it was a lovely place to spend the summer, with the Danube and the beautiful garden.

On the evening to which Mr Lietzen's daughter had referred, the family had invited guests for dinner. They were to eat wild boar *en daube*. The table on the Danube-facing terrace had been elegantly set for ten or twelve people. There were great bunches of flowers on the table and above it, under the bright electric lamps, suspended on wires, were newly purchased bright green insect nets, waiting for their haul of inevitable prey. The debates about the menu which had preceded the dinner—considering that a cabinet minister was among the guests—had lasted for days and had ended in triumph for Cook. This redoubtable lady, who wore spectacles for cooking and was known as 'Professor' by the family on account of it, had got her way: she was to serve wild boar braised in red wine.

Cook ('Professor') had been campaigning for this for some time. On occasion she had even resorted to pleading, assuring her mistress that wild boar *en daube* was her star turn, the pinnacle of her achievement—and yet somehow, unaccountably, it was a part she had never been called upon to perform for the Lietzens. And just like an actress, who will stake her whole career on securing a single role, she began to make a scene, even to the point of bursting into tears. Her melodramatic gestures and beseeching countenance would have been better suited to the words 'I beg you to cast me as Mary Queen of Scots' than to the four syllables she kept coming back to: 'wild boar *en daube*'. Eventually the silver-haired Mrs Lietzen gave in.

'Very well, we look forward to the performance.'

The small party of guests had arrived hungry and were served generous quantities of iced vermouth before dinner. When dinner stubbornly failed to appear, it began to be suspected that something was amiss. Mrs Lietzen even went down to the kitchen—something she had never been known to do before. She reappeared wreathed in smiles.

'Do take your seats.'

The wild boar was brought in. Word had got out about it some days ago and the anticipation was palpable.

It was bad. It was execrable. In fact—not to beat about the bush—it was inedible. There was nothing that anyone could say in its defence. First the guests and then the hosts set down their knives and forks in mute defeat. Stephen Lietzen found this unanimous surrender rather amusing but his wife had turned pale. It was quite clear what had happened, and in the circumstances perfectly understandable. 'Professor' had had an attack of stage fright and had messed up her lines. The guests were terribly nice about it. They found the whole thing rather funny and laughed at poor Mrs Lietzen's discomfiture. And what happened next was the kind of thing entirely suited to a man of Mr Lietzen's easy-going disposition: an impromptu supper.

'Just bring out everything we've got,' he said.

A great flurry ensued. Mother, daughter and Mr Lietzen's secretary all began scurrying around, fetching and carrying. One might have expected to learn that while all this was going on, Cook was lying sprawled on the kitchen floor in a dead faint or that she had slit her wrists with the bread knife. But no. At this moment of crisis, she showed her true mettle, putting her shoulder valiantly to the wheel to save what could be saved of the situation. The little village girls, who worked for the Lietzens as maids, ran down to the cellar, out to the larder, eagerly ferrying things to and fro. A huge goose liver—another of Cook's *tours de force*, though much less famous than her wild boar *en daube*—was lifted out of its deep vat of whey and set on the stove to simmer. The hens were awakened from their unsuspecting slumbers and tossed into frying pans before they could so much as utter a peep. When they came to be served, they were a little bloody around the joints and the salad dressing was a touch too vinegary—but this could be taken as a symptom, for the benefit of those around the table, of Cook's flustered state. The guests drowned these minor errors in wine. A very great deal was drunk. And to finish off, yellow raspberries were served. Yellow raspberries have a far subtler taste and scent than red ones. They did a great deal to lift the mood.

There were only two young people among the guests: Miss Lietzen and the family secretary. The rest of the company, beginning with the cabinet minister, were elderly gentlemen, and there were one or two elderly ladies as well. The dinner had been convened in order to discuss the problem of rogue rowers. All the guests had properties near the river and as far as they were concerned, rogue rowers were to the water what mosquitoes are to the air: a Danube curse. Most of those present had built their houses on the waterfront and for them the misery began every Saturday afternoon. By Sunday it had become unbearable. For the riverside householder, a rogue rower is the enemy incarnate. He ties up his boat, he lights a camp fire, he starts cooking over it, he begs a bit of cooking oil from the householder's kitchens, or water from his pump (which admittedly is preferable to asking for oil), he leaves greaseproof salami wrappings strewn behind him, he steals flowers from the garden and—*le plus horrible*—lounges about all afternoon naked, sometimes even shamelessly canoodling on the foreshore...

It was not long before these rowers were being spoken of with such inchoate rage that an impartial listener could have been forgiven for getting the parts muddled up and thinking that this was a battle between rogue landowners and peace-loving rowers. But the bluster was not of long duration because sure enough, inexorably, the conversation began moving from rogue rowing to general politics. Lietzen's guests were interested in what their host had to say. Even the cabinet minister paid careful attention. Lietzen had been a member of parliament before the war. He had been one of Tisza's[5] most fervent supporters (though in party circles what was more famous was how little Tisza had returned the compliment). Here though, down on the Danube, Lietzen was popular. He was clever, he always had some scheme afoot. And he was always shifting great volumes of money around. He assiduously and tactfully cultivated a good rapport with his neighbours. The neighbours appreciated this and were forever finding things to sell to him: a lame old horse for an exorbitant sum; a dinner service (a bit chipped here and there, it was true, but still genuine Herend porcelain); a couple of barrels of wine (even sourer than the stuff he produced himself); an original sketch by Munkácsy[6], so blackened and foxed that it was impossible to tell whether it was of a young horse-tamer drinking at an inn or an old widow mourning her dead husband. Lietzen knew full well what he was buying. He never haggled, he just laughed and took whatever he was offered, maintaining that 'my relationship with my neighbours is sacrosanct.' And whenever the opportunity arose, he entertained those same neighbours, feeding and watering them with little luxuries that were never known to appear at their own tables: langoustines and French champagne. So all in all, Lietzen was well liked. Everyone was fond of him. Everyone, that is, except Tisza. But never mind: Lietzen had outlived that particular tricky customer, and after a while people stopped asking him about it. There is a lot to be said for outliving people.

At eleven o'clock everyone left the terrace and went down into the garden, where wine had been set out under the big walnut tree. There was coffee on the table and, in a capacious ice bucket, Mumm champagne, the famous *cordon rouge* of its label clearly visible. The cabinet minister always cut his with Parád[7] mineral water, a form of sacrilege that—as he liked to point out—would cost even the most saccharine of suitors the chance of old Mumm's daughter's hand in marriage.

The night air was beautifully mild. They drank. They talked politics, loudly, emphatically and vinously. The two young people sat some distance apart, listening. The secretary paid keen attention to what was said but offered no remark of his own. The girl smiled, but she was not bored. She stood up, lingered a little at the table, then slowly began to walk away down the dark garden. Her mother watched her as she went.

'Where are you going?'

The girl turned back. 'Just down to the Danube for a bit.' She saw that the secretary was looking at her. 'Come with me,' she said softly.

The secretary stood up, excused himself and obediently hurried after her. The girl's white dress glimmered against the dark trees. When he caught up with her, she set off wordlessly down the garden. Just for something to say, the secretary said,

'Going down to the Danube?'

'Yes.'

'What do you want to do there?'

'Nothing.'

She had never asked the secretary to go anywhere with her before. She had barely spoken to him. The 'Daddy's secretary' type of man is barely a human being as far as certain sorts of young lady are concerned. The 'Daddy's secretary' type, with his big leather briefcase, bows deferentially if he bumps into her in the house, and the young lady inclines her head with a stiff little smile. 'Daddy's secretary' never exchanges pleasantries with the daughter of his esteemed employer. 'Daddy's secretary' always hurries on his way. He appears, he bows, he doesn't stop, he hurries off. And the following day he appears again, and bows again, and hurries off again. The truth of it is that 'Daddy's secretary' has no interest in his employer's daughter.

They walked down to the end of the dark garden, then

through the little iron gate and down a couple of steps into the orchard. The secretary felt ill at ease, not knowing what on earth to say to this girl, with whom he had so far exchanged no more than a 'Good morning' or 'Good afternoon'.

'It's a lovely evening.'

The girl laughed. 'Is that all?'

'No, no, I really mean it. I'm not just saying it to be polite. It really is one of the nicest evenings so far this summer...'

The girl was still laughing. 'Not just to be polite, you say?'

'Yes.'

She stopped laughing. 'I'm sorry. You think I'm tipsy, don't you?'

'No, of course not.'

'Oh yes you do!'

They were making their way through the orchard now, past small, overloaded apricot trees. Their branches were bowed so low that one almost felt sorry for them.

'They're like all those poor women with too many children,' the girl said.

The secretary looked at the trees more closely.

'What an excellent metaphor.'

'I wouldn't say excellent,' said the girl. She looked at him and went on, 'It's not excellent at all, Mr Szabó. It's good enough, I suppose, but let's not exaggerate.'

They had reached the tomato beds. The girl's manner

annoyed the secretary. He was nearing the end of his tenure with Mr Lietzen, who had found him a job with a bank in Milan. He had plenty to preoccupy him. Somehow or other he had to make sure that his mother would be taken care of. And there were one or additions he was going to need to make to his wardrobe. And on top of all that, he was spending several hours a day refreshing and perfecting his Italian. He was on his way to a new world, a whole new life among complete strangers. Before he went there were various bills to be settled, an instalment to be paid off here and there, and then the worry of making sure that money for all the future instalments would be forthcoming from Milan, and after that from Venice. The girl's words rang in his ears. 'Let's not exaggerate.' The careless, twitting words of a rich young lady without a worry in the world. It annoyed him.

They were passing the melon beds now. The melons slumbered sweetly on the soft ground, quilted among their large leaves. The girl spoke again.

'Didn't you have anything to drink at all?'

'No.'

'Are you the kind that rarely does?'

'Yes.'

'Do you know the German word "*einsilbig*"?'

'I can translate it.'

'That's not enough. You need to understand it. It's the sort of word people use to describe men like you, men who give one-syllable answers to everything. *Ja, nein.* If my company bores you so horribly, then...

'What makes you think that?'

'You make it perfectly obvious.'

The secretary made no reply. He continued walking beside Miss Lietzen in silence. But she would not allow him to stay silent for long.

'What's your first name?'

'Aurelian.'

His voice was a little resentful. She laughed.

'Why are you laughing?'

'Because I already knew.'

He could tell that she was bored. She was teasing him, not unkindly, but as a way of making things livelier between them. She was taking it too far, though.

'I think secretaries are selfish people,' she was saying. 'They don't like being out at night among the melon beds with their employers' daughters.'

'I wouldn't say that. Why should a secretary not like such a thing?'

'Because secretaries are cautious, always on their guard. Secretaries have to worry about their daily bread. I've never heard of a secretary who was willing to take a risk. I think secretaries are cowards.'

The young man stopped. 'What did you say?'

The girl didn't stop. Continuing on her way she said, lightly tossing the word over her shoulder,

'Nothing.'

Aurelian was quite angry by now. Not very angry, but still, he was rather beginning to hate this impertinent, beautiful young girl. But what did it matter? She was bored, she had had a glass or two of champagne. And in a week's time he would be on a train to Milan.

They left the melon beds and walked down to the edge of the main road. It ran right along the waterfront, following the Danube. A new moon and a few stars were shining faintly, a soft milky white. The acacia trees that lined both sides of the road were white too, with dust. A car raced past. The pale road and the dust-covered trees glimmered and quivered before it, in the probing trail of its advancing headlights. Then there was silence. From far away, somewhere in the village, came the barely audible sound of a radio. They crossed the road and went down towards the river, to where the Lietzens' little bathing hut and rowing boat were. It was some distance from the road to the water's edge.

The girl stopped. 'I'm tired,' she said simply. 'I'd like you to carry me.' She laughed up at Aurelian's astonished face.

Aurelian didn't understand. 'What did you say?'

'I'd like you to carry me. Pick me up and carry me. Or don't you dare?'

She was putting on the charm now. A little startled by her own idea, but unwilling to relinquish it, she said again, a little hesitantly, 'Don't you dare?'

Aurelian looked at her for a moment, assessed her with

his eyes, in the way a gymnast assesses the apparatus before he starts, then picked her up. Slowly he carried her down the grassy bank, through the tangle of bushes. He didn't say a word. The girl laid her head on his left arm. Aurelian's right hand was holding her at the knee. Her body was supple, slender and nicely formed. She smelled like fresh bread. She looked up into his eyes and said teasingly,

'Am I heavy?'

'No.'

'Because I asked you to carry me but you aren't. You're *lugging* me.'

Aurelian stopped to catch his breath and looked down into her wide, laughing eyes. 'Don't make fun of me or I'll drop you.'

'No you won't!'

He set off with her again. He could see the water shining through the bushes.

The girl kept on looking into his eyes with that same faint, wistful little smile. She felt a sort of tiptoeing, tentative tenderness, that seemed to dart in and out of her, but then she settled down instead to imagine that she was being rescued from something.

'Run!' she cried. 'Save me!'

'From what?'

'From fire, from flood—what do I know?' She was suddenly, irrationally happy.

Aurelian did not run, but he did quicken his pace as

he continued with her towards the water. She was staring at him quite openly now, at his downcast eyes, at the play of muscle in his arms, noting the way his heart throbbed under his white shirt when he stopped to catch his breath. But she was saved by her two glasses of champagne from getting too deeply immersed in forbidden fantasies. Instead, her tipsiness took her back to the foolish notion that she was being 'saved' from a burning house by a strong man. She closed her eyes with a blissful smile.

From high above them, from the house came a long-drawn-out cry of maternal concern.

'I-i-irma-a-a!'

How many times had Irma Lietzen heard that cry, in the happy days of her childhood? From the water's edge, she sent up a correspondingly elongated response.

'Co-o-om-i-ing!'

It was a brief, primeval form of wireless exchange. A mother communicating with her child, her meaning unambiguous, her message freighted with something that transcends mere information. Such messages are always the same, in every circumstance in which they are deployed. Their substance never changes. They breathe fresh vigour, each time they are repeated, into the immutability of the family bond.

Very carefully, Aurelian put the girl down and they set off back up the little path between the slumbering melons. He made a deliberate effort to hide his heavy breathing and

Irma, as she walked beside him, clutched his arm and laid her head against his shoulder. She said nothing. When the guests came into view, still sitting drinking wine under the walnut tree in the light of the hanging lantern with the red shade, she dropped the secretary's arm and ran ahead, cutting across the mown grass.

'Trampling on the lawn again!' tutted her mother reproachfully.

Aurelian came slowly after her, keeping to the gravel that skirted the oval lawn.

And that was all there was to it.

The guests were eating toast. Flustered Cook had finally found her equilibrium. The toast was excellent: neither soggy nor desiccated, not too thick nor too thin, neither underdone nor burnt. The *artiste* who had been a flop as Mary Queen of Scots had now found a walk-on part in which to star unconditionally.

Irma came to a stop beside her mother, bent down to embrace her, burying her face in her luxuriant white hair. Aurelian took a seat close by. Nobody noticed them; the guests were all locked in heated argument. In the centre of the table sat a huge platter of fragrant golden toast. Mrs Lietzen picked up a fork and pointed it at her daughter.

'Want some?'

'Absolutely! I love toast.'

'Not "I love". You mean, "Yes please".'

Irma looked a question at Aurelian.

'No thank you,' he said, flushing a little.

So no toast for him. The guests by this time were bellowing politics. Aurelian stared at the tablecloth. Later, one of the guests gave him a lift back to Budapest in his motor car. Irma did not see him for a week after that, and even then only for ten minutes, when he came to say goodbye to her mother, the day before he left for Italy.

That had been exactly two years ago.

3

Upstairs in a Venice hotel room, with a palatially too-high ceiling and palatial gold wallpaper, at half past eleven in the morning, a middle-aged lady with snow-white hair lay in a palatially wide bed with black and gold carved bedposts, under an over-opulent chandelier of antique Murano glass. Above her head rose a white lace canopy, falling in rich folds and draped across the whole width of the bed. Its purpose was to keep out the mosquitoes but it now served to heighten the impression of the white-haired lady's lying in state. The door into the living-room stood open. The lady in the bed turned towards the window, looked out at the sky for a while, then called faintly,

'Judith!'

A beautiful dark-haired girl came in from the living-room and bent dutifully over the bed.

'You called, Ma'am?'

'Open the window, please. I don't think I'll get up today.'

The dark-haired girl opened the window, admitting the fresh breeze and the hubbub of the Grand Canal into the most expensive room of this five-hundred-year-old *palazzo*-turned-hotel.

'Where is Irma?'

'I think she went for out for a short walk before lunch.'

'And my husband?'

'He went with her.'

'Thank you.'

The dark-haired girl went back to the living-room and went on reading her book in her chair by the window. The Lietzens' suite comprised four rooms in all. Beyond the living-room was Irma's bedroom, and opening off Mrs Lietzen's bedroom was the room where Mr Lietzen slept. Across the corridor, a little further away, was a fifth room, much plainer than the others. This belonged to the beautiful dark-haired girl, Mrs Lietzen's nurse. There was a sixth room too, but it was not in Venice. It was in Mestre, at the Hotel Zordan. That was where the chauffeur was staying, next to the garage, so as to be close to the seventh room, officially called the 'box', where the motor car was kept. The chauffeur went there every day at noon, to 'groom the horse', as he put it, to brush it, feed and water it and to check its hooves. The Lietzens lived in style. No family from their region of the Danube basin put on a better show. Lietzen had no fortune of his own; like most speculators he aimed to tie down his fickle wealth in the jewellery he gave his wife. His income was immense but he was wayward with it. As soon as he came into any money, he spent it all on his wife and daughter. Just at the moment he was rather short, although 'rather short' in Lietzen's case was still great riches by any ordinary standards. For Lietzen, having 'no money' meant that he had plenty but it was not a state of affairs that could be trusted to continue.

'Judith?'

The dark-haired girl put her book down again and once more presented herself in the white-haired lady's bedroom.

'You called, Ma'am?'

'Close the window, please.'

Judith did so. 'Will there be anything else?' She waited patiently for further orders.

'Nothing, thank you.'

The girl retreated, took up her place at the window again and read some more of her book.

Judith was a trained nurse. Someone from a good family had been needed to look after Mrs Lietzen and Judith had been recommended by the wife of a government secretary. Mrs Lietzen had had a difficult operation and was recuperating rather slowly. There was even a suspicion—no more than a very faint one—that, like so many ladies who have undergone difficult operations, she had found a friend in morphine. Mrs Lietzen needed a lot of looking after. She had reached that age when ladies begin to lose their calm and level-headedness, when suddenly, for no reason at all, they either burst laughing or burst into tears, when they toy with thoughts of suicide, suffering to the bitter end that mysterious, turbulent storm which nature wreaks on them as it brings their reproductive years to a close. Mrs Lietzen was well over fifty.

'Judith!'

'You called, Ma'am?'

'Thank you. I don't need anything. I just wanted to make sure you were there.'

Judith had originally planned to study medicine but had barely embarked on her degree when her father, scion of a highly respectable family, was found dead in his office, slumped in his chair. In front of him on the desk were sixteen letters, their envelopes all addressed, and on the floor next to his chair a little Browning handgun. He had been the head of a small state-owned concern and had found himself unable to account for a large sum of money. Even now it was not clear where the poor man had put the money because he and his daughter lived very modestly. Judith never went back to her university. Her mother had died many years ago. A relative in Vienna gave her a roof over her head and it was there that she got her nursing license. She never wanted to go back to Budapest, where everyone knew her family. Even though her father, who had been an honest and upstanding man, had been forgiven, Judith did not want anyone to feel sorry for her. The government secretary who had recommended her mentioned that the Lietzens were looking for a nurse to accompany them on a trip abroad. Judith had met the Lietzens at the Sacher Hotel in Vienna and agreed to take on the job. Mr Lietzen was extremely pleased with her, for precisely the reason that his wife was not: Judith was thorough and impassive. She took her work very seriously, she was day and night at Mrs Lietzen's beck and call. But there was something hard about her. She could never assume that mask of feigned tenderness which comes so naturally to nurses whose fathers have not shot themselves, girls who have risen to nursing rather than sunk to it and who speak to their patients in the first person plural ('My word, we *did* sleep well, didn't we?'). Judith had no talent for that sort of thing. So Mrs Lietzen didn't like her, because Mrs Lietzen liked everything to be sweet and fluffy and Judith wasn't. There was nothing sweet and fluffy about her beauty, either. Her figure was perfect without being sensual. She had a slightly deliberate way of walking and the way she dressed took the 'plenty of black and not much white' dictum rather too far. Nor was there any sweetness in her eyes. In fact, there was something else in them entirely: they were full of poetry. The Lietzens had come to describe her eyes as 'Ottoman'. The eyeballs were a bluish milky white, the irises a very deep black, lying closer to the upper eyelid than the lower, a feature which gave her eyes a look of slumbrous passion, cast into dreamy shadow by long, thick lashes. Keen readers of novels would see in such a gaze the 'captive odalisque staring into the moonlight with untamed yearning, from behind the bars of her harem window'. That is what made the Lietzen ladies say that Judith had 'Ottoman' eyes.

'Judith!'

'You called, Ma'am?'

The white-haired lady sat up in bed. 'Give me my red hat, please.'

Judith fetched the red hat from the wardrobe, as if the request were as natural as her mistress asking for her pills.

'And now the big mirror, please. Hold it for a moment so I can look.'

The little scarlet hat at once took twenty years off the white-haired lady. There she sat, propped up in bed in her nightgown, with the red hat perched on her carefully contrived white curls. She adjusted it, turning her head this way and that in the mirror, then smiling in loving satisfaction at the reflection that stared back out at her. Perhaps she was expecting a 'How well it becomes you, Ma'am,' or a 'Oh, how perfectly it sets off your hair,' but Judith said nothing. And yet if it had been required, she would patiently have stood holding the heavy silver-framed mirror in front of her mistress for a full hour or more.

Mr Lietzen, at that moment, was with his daughter, sitting downstairs in the hotel bar on a wide leather couch. He was drinking a dry Martini and had ordered a glass of sweet Italian vermouth for her. He loved this sort of thing: sitting in a bar, wetting his whistle with the daughter he adored. She was his only child and because he so seldom found time to be with her, he tended to indulge her. Her mother's love was often of the 'no you mayn't' kind. The word 'mayn't' was foreign to Mr Lietzen's vocabulary. In fact, there had been times—when the maternal 'mayn't' had seemed unnecessarily harsh—when Mr Lietzen had winked at Irma behind her mother's back as if to say, 'Don't take it seriously, just let her rattle on.' He was a dapper man, younger-looking than his sixty years. There was something slightly English in his appearance. In Budapest, people said he looked like a British milord, though in fact his Englishness was of the kind that is far more frequently seen in a member of the lower house. A true English lord, Lord Derby for instance, has nothing about him that can be classed as classically English. In fact, the Lord Derbys of this world look disappointingly like provincial Hungarian justices of the peace.

Any stranger who saw Mr Lietzen and Irma sitting in the hotel bar would never have guessed that they were father and daughter. The daughter looked so brightly and eagerly at the father, and the father was so deferent and benevolent and twinkling with the girl, that any stranger passing by would have had nothing but pity for him, a poor old fool who had clearly fallen into the clutches of a schemer.

The old fool went up to the counter to pay for their drinks. He counted out the necessary notes, put the rest away, and went back to his daughter.

'Give me your hand, Irmie.'

The girl did so, and felt a tightly folded wad of paper being pressed into her palm.

'What's this?'

'Don't let go of me,' said Mr Lietzen. 'Your hand is so

small that people will see. Put it in your bag.'

Irma laughed and tucked the money away. 'Darling Daddy! Thank you.'

'You can have a look when you get upstairs. It's a thousand. A thousand *lire*.'

Irma gaped at him. 'I thought you were going to say a hundred.'

'No, my dear, a thousand. I've got to go away, you see, to Milan and Genoa. I might not see you for weeks. So—well, let's just say it's something to remember me by. But don't go spending it in dribs and drabs like you usually do. I've given you a great big whack so you can buy something really nice for yourself. One single big thing. Something you really, truly want. Something special. Is there anything you have in mind? Something really Venetian?'

'A mirror, perhaps. The mirrors are divine.'

'All right, it could be a mirror, that's fine by me. Just don't rush into anything, there's plenty of time. Wait till you see something you really want. And don't keep describing everything as "divine".'

She kissed her father's hand. She felt she almost had tears in her eyes. It had been such typical male gesture on his part and it made her a little sad. 'Daddy only knows how to love me through money,' she thought. Crude though it had been, Mr Lietzen's gesture had been one of complete sincerity—a token of remorse. He tried so hard and yet despite his sixty years he was so childishly simple. His daughter, left so much to her own devices, was deeply moved.

Mr Lietzen got up, took Irma by the arm and walked with her towards the lift.

'We'll have lunch upstairs in the room. Your mother will like that because she's been cooped up in bed all day. And don't be sad to see me go. If things go well in Milan and Genoa there'll be money to show for it. Lots of money. I'm exporting to India now. If I told you *what* I was exporting you'd laugh your head off.'

'Tell me!' giggled Irma. 'I've started laughing already.'

"Certainly not!' Mr Lietzen looked at his watch. 'One minute to midday,' he said. 'Your mother's daily torture is about to begin.'

Hardly had he said so when midday burst upon them. Midday is the reason why no one's watch tells the wrong time in Venice. At twelve noon precisely, the tranquil midday quiet is rent asunder by cannon fire, loud enough to set the glasses rattling on all the luncheon tables. And at the same time, the hideous wail of the Arsenale siren starts up and the bronze hammers of the Orologio beat twelve. The huge bells in St Mark's Campanile start to swing and the bells in all the bell-towers of all the other churches—and there are some eighty-five of them in Venice—take up the clamour too, lustily tolling noon. It is impossible not to reset one's watch.

The living-room table was already laid for luncheon when they got upstairs. The red hat had long been put back in the wardrobe. The window was open again and the white-haired lady, lying back against her pillows amid the froth of the lace canopy, was still recovering from the cannon fire. She looked across at them, a pained expression on her lightly made-up face. Weakly, amid the barrage of the bells, she held out a pale white hand, its fingernails carefully lacquered in dark red.

After lunch they left Mrs Lietzen to sleep. Judith went to her room and Irma and her father conversed in whispers in the living-room. They wanted Mrs Lietzen to rest so that in the afternoon she would have the strength to go out in a gondola with her new friend Mrs Lineman. Mrs Lietzen's lust for life—as demonstrated by the episode with the red hat—was slowly returning after her lengthy illness. Since the day before yesterday she even had a friend, this Mrs Lineman, an elderly American widow, whom Mrs Lietzen had met in the hotel lobby. They had already played bridge together and Mrs Lietzen was altogether rather taken with her new acquaintance. The *coup de foudre* of love at first sight, brought to the world's attention by Romeo and Juliet and later by Louis XV and Madame Dubarry, but which occurs so rarely among the young, is rather common in elderly ladies, particularly when they are holidaying abroad in the summer. Only yesterday Mrs Lietzen and Mrs Lineman had gone out in a gondola together and they were planning to go again that afternoon. Life was beginning to seem worth living. Mrs Lietzen adored tittle-tattle—only when it concerned people of blue blood, of course—and Mrs Lineman had been coming to Venice for years. She loved the city, she knew it very well. In the early years she had rented a *palazzo* but now she had taken to staying in an hotel, though her wealth was in no way diminished. She had a passion for Venetian cuisine. She knew all the quaint traditional dishes and was addicted to eating them—and inviting others to do so—in out-of-the-way taverns. But an even greater passion than this was the enthusiasm she nurtured for the Venetian aristocracy. From their gondola she had pointed out all the *palazzi* to Mrs Lietzen, telling her who lived in which and what kinds of things they ate. She promised to get Mrs Lietzen an *entrée* into close-knit family circles. She would take her to a musical *soirée* at the Princesse de Polignac's[8]. She would secure her an invitation to the ancient and wealthy Dolfin Boldùs. In fact she would even contrive that Mrs Lietzen be asked to take tea by Countess Morosini, who not so long ago had been the most beautiful woman in Venice and who regularly gave tea to kings and emperors in her *palazzo*—the very *palazzo* where Mrs Lietzen would soon drink tea herself. This was quite a thing, although according to Mrs Lineman the Countess was only from a minor branch of the great family whose forebear, Francesco Morosini, had been the hammer of the Turks. In fact, she went on—'and as a Hungarian you will be interested in this,'—a daughter of the main branch of the family, the beautiful Tommasina Morosini, had been the mother of the last Hungarian king of the House of Arpad, Andrew III[9], and in addition—'which as a Hungarian you will also find fascinating,'—as the mother of a Hungarian king it was she who had introduced the concept of Hungarian goulash to Venice, a dish which still existed in the guise of *cavromàn in umido*. 'You can read all about it in Zorzi's book on Venetian cuisine.'

A noble family tree and bourgeois cookery! Mrs Lietzen, 'as a Hungarian', was certainly fascinated by both these things. She was quite carried away by the world that seemed to be opening up before her. It was undoubtedly at the root of her improved health. Mrs Lineman, they all agreed, was a blessing. She was nothing like as handsome a matron as Mother. Quite the contrary, she was short and stocky, with bright eyes peering out from behind a pair of *pince-nez*, and was only truly at her best when she was being spoken to, because then she concentrated so hard that her nose began to twitch and her lip curled and her beady eyes behind the *pince-nez* seemed to say, 'What's that funny smell?' If on the other hand it was Mrs Lineman doing the talking, she lowered her head and fixed her interlocutor with her eyes over the rim of her glasses and smiled and moved her mouth so fast that it looked like a little electric engine, which tended to make Mrs Lietzen rather nervous.

'A small price to pay,' was Mr Lietzen's verdict. 'At least your poor dear mother will have company when I've gone to Milan…' He looked at his watch. 'I think I'll go to my room. I've got a lot of work to do. What are your plans?'

'I'm going to St Mark's Square.'

Lietzen went to his room. Irma stood for a moment in front of the mirror, then snatched up her bag and hurried out. She had not seen Aurelian for two days. He had given no sign of life yesterday. Perhaps now he might be sitting outside Florian's. She knew he was free around midday. Her introduction to Venice was progressing horribly slowly; she would have to work out some kind of system with him. He was the only person she could talk to, after all. She didn't know a single other soul here. She realised how impatient she was, how quickly she was hurrying to get to the lift. How interesting, she thought. I seem to want to devour Venice all at once.

The lift didn't come the first time. She pressed the button again, lengthily, about four times. He'll be off back to the bank any minute and I'll be left alone in that great big square, she told herself fretfully. She crossed the lobby. Two good-looking young people were sitting next to each other, fast asleep in big armchairs. An English honeymoon couple. There were empty cocktail glasses in front of both of them. He was so young he might still have been a sixth-former and she looked like a typical schoolgirl. They were known and liked in the hotel. Two wealthy English families, impatient to unite their respective fortunes, had wed these two children to each other. They had come to Venice on their honeymoon and all they seemed to do was sleep. If the concierge saw one of the guests marvelling at it, he would say conspiratorially,

'*Viaggio di nozze.*' Irma stopped to look for a moment at the two little slumbering faces. The young bride seemed to sense that she was being watched. She opened her eyes and turned to her husband.

'Fred!'

He stirred and opened his eyes in turn. 'Bunny?'

'Wake up!'

Irma hurried away. Within a minute the young couple, Fred and Bunny, had fallen asleep again, like babies sleeping side by side in matching cots.

Irma realised once again that she was rushing. Her footfalls sounded too eager under the echoing arcade of the Doge's Palace. Shaking her head she slowed down. Why am I in such a hurry? she asked herself. I need to take my time. She stood still for a moment. My parents were already middle-aged when I was born, she thought, and they say that the children of such parents tend to be healthy and well-balanced, classic examples of poise and self-possession. So it's odd that I should be so highly strung. Or is it just now that I'm like this?

In the sweltering midday heat, St Mark's Square was empty. Opposite the Basilica the pigeons were cooling themselves, high up among the reliefs and cornices of the Procurazie Nuove's long frieze. Hundreds and hundreds of black dots were strung out along the white marble. In front of Florian's, great awnings were slung between the columns and it was only there, under their shade, that any movement was to be seen. Close to one of the columns, in a position which commanded a clear view over the Piazza, Aurelian was sitting alone. The column cast its shade across his chair. Irma had spotted him some time ago, as she made her way across the square in front of the row of shops. She brought herself to an abrupt halt in front of one of the window displays and mindlessly began looking at a dark blue wine set, a decanter and six glasses, all of them with wide, rippling, gilded rims. What was she in such a hurry for?

A pretty girl came to the shop door and addressed Irma in German.

'*Wollen Sie das Geschäft besichtigen?*'

'*Danke, nein.*'

'*Alles echt böhmisches Glas.*'[10]

It was safe to move on now. Shall I stop at another window? she wondered. She decided there was no need. She made her way towards where Aurelian was sitting, a small smile playing about her lips. That will make a good first topic of conversation, she thought. The fact that shops in Venice all sell Bohemian crystal. That's like a wine cellar in Tokaj[11] serving German Riesling. Making to look as if she had only just noticed him, she began waving at Aurelian with her handbag. She came to a halt beside his table.

'What are you doing here?'

'Waiting for half past two. That's when I have to be back at the bank.'

'I'm doing a bit of shopping.'

'In this heat? Why don't you sit down for a while?'

'All right, but just for a minute or two.'

She took a seat where she could look out at the Piazza and the Basilica. 'I'll sit here, where I can see my lovely golden angels.'

The waiter came and hovered in front of her inquiringly, hiding her lovely golden angels. Irma smiled across at Aurelian proudly.

'I know. *Caffè in ghiaccio.*'

He shook his head. 'Quite wrong, I'm afraid.'

'What, then?'

'Warm *espresso.*'

'In this heat?'

'Exactly. That's the rule when it's hot.'

The waiter retreated, revealing the golden angels once more.

'I've learned something new again.'

Leaning towards her, Aurelian said, very softly, 'Won't you tell me who the man was who taught you about the Dolomites and gentlemen's tailors in Madrid?'

'No.'

'What else did he teach you?'

'Oh, lots of things. For example—and you might find this useful—that when you're mixing Gorgonzola with butter, you should add a dash of Worcestershire sauce. No more than a couple of drops. Once you know that, you won't forget.'

'Well, that has given me a clue,' said Aurelian. 'He can't have been a very young man if he was talking to you about cookery.'

The Orologio bell clanged noisily, twice. The pigeons all reacted *en masse*, all hundred thousand of them (or perhaps a million), madly taking to the sky at the sound of the clock, then settling in another corner of the square like a great black storm cloud.

'Feeding time,' Aurelian explained.

From the corner behind the further arcades came a man in a street-sweeper's uniform. He had been standing there for some minutes, by one of the columns, waiting for the clock to chime. He had a sack in his hand, which he opened and then set off across the Piazza, trailing the big open bag behind him. As it regurgitated its contents, the pigeons' excitement was explained. The man with the sack traced a big letter S across the square in grains of corn, then left. The pigeons jostled frantically over the great mass of maize, mercilessly pecking each other out of the way. The saddest thing was a sight one always sees on occasions like this: there is always one bird that finds itself so pushed and shoved by the others that it gives up the struggle, detaches itself from the dense black flock and gloomily takes itself off to strut around alone in a distant corner. Or else it comes to rest a little further off and glares glassily at its gorging fellows.

Aurelian explained all this to Irma.

'I feel I should apologise,' she said, 'for taking up so much of your time. I feel I must be becoming a burden to you.'

'Not at all…'

'I am sure you have other things you could be doing.'

'Not really.'

'Oh, come now!'

'No, truly.'

Irma felt a little vexed. 'It's extraordinary how little I know about you. Here we are, sitting in St Mark's Square, and it's as if you had done nothing at all for the past two years but sit here, silent and solitary, waiting for the chance to talk about pigeon-feeding time to—to a Hungarian tourist. You give absolutely nothing away.'

'There is nothing *to* give away.'

'Oh for Heaven's sake, there must be, don't be silly! You are so—how shall I put it—so *impersonal* with me. I don't know why I bother coming to seek you out.'

'You came to seek me out? You told me you were doing a bit of shopping.'

'Well, that's true, but… All right, I don't know why I sat down at your table, then. Perhaps—perhaps I have too much faith in my own instincts.'

'I don't know what you mean.'

She blushed a little, then quietly, almost crossly, tried to explain. 'Two years ago, in Tahifalu, I—I asked you to go down to the Danube with me. There was no reason for my doing so. I didn't like you, I didn't need you, you weren't a friend, you weren't handsome or rich. It was just instinct…'

'I…'

'And it must have been a good idea because I was still a child at the time so I had instincts I could trust. But now my power to judge has been ruined by the fact that I've started to think about things more deeply. The trouble is, though, I'm not clever enough for deep thoughts.'

'I'm sure that's not true. What are you thinking now, for instance?'

'That sitting here with you and looking at you, I realise that you still aren't handsome, or rich, or my friend, and that I don't like you and don't need you.'

Aurelian swallowed. 'There you are, you see,' he said.

Irma sensed that she had overstepped an invisible mark. She fell silent, staring at the hundreds of empty chairs and tables almost melting in the sunshine.

'How many chairs are there outside Florian's?'

'Nine hundred and eighty.'

'That's the one reassuring thing about you, I think. You count everything.'

'I didn't count the chairs.'

'How do you know, then?'

'I once asked the same question. Of the head waiter.'

'Have I upset you?'

Aurelian shook his head with a deprecating smile. Irma stared into her empty coffee cup, concentrating very hard on trying to extract a remaining grain of sugar with her spoon. Then suddenly she pushed the cup away.

'In the hotel,' she said, 'I saw a little child with a bunch of thin, white strands of something. It looked just like a lock of silvery hair. It was soft and pliable like hair, too, but I was told it was made of glass and that they make it in a workshop somewhere near here. Have you heard of it?'

Aurelian laughed. 'You'll tease me for being a tour guide again, but yes. They don't call it glass hair, they call it glass wool, *lana di vetro*. They make it just over there, on the other side of that alleyway.' He pointed.

'I knew you'd know. One can always come to you with questions like that. I'd like to go and look. Will you take me?'

'My pleasure. Waiter!'

They waited for the bill in silence. Irma kept her eyes fixed on the Basilica roof while Aurelian paid, and even after he got up and indicated that he was ready to go, she still did not move.

'What are you staring at so hard?'

'I'm staring at the angel's golden wing until it moves. It always works. I made it move the day before yesterday too. Only then you didn't notice that I was doing it and you didn't ask me what I was staring at so hard.'

'Let's go,' Aurelian said, making to shepherd her away.

They went through a columned entranceway, making for the narrow alley where the glass wool workshop was.

On their way, they passed a scruffy half-basement fitted up as a forge, with no panes in the windows, through whose stout, rusty iron bars you could peer in across a mass of scrap metal to see two half-naked men, one of them using tongs to hold a piece of molten iron on an anvil while the other pummelled it with a hammer, sending out showers of hissing sparks. Aurelian stopped by the window and called out in Hungarian:

'*Adj' isten!*'

The man with the hammer grinned, his teeth bright white in his sooty, grimy face. '*Jó napot kívánok!*'[12]

'The blacksmith is Hungarian,' Aurelian explained, as they went on their way. 'Once, as I was coming past here, I heard someone singing in Hungarian. Just imagine, singing in that fiery, dark hole. I got into conversation with him and we've been good friends ever since. He came here as a prisoner of war and ended up staying.'

'Poor fellow,' said Irma and went back to the window. 'I say!', she called out, then grabbed all the cigarettes she had and shoved them at him through the window bars.

The deafening noise of the forge ceased for a moment. Then the hammer crashed down again.

'Just one more thing,' she said, running back yet again to the cellar window. She shouted to make herself heard above the din of the hammer: 'Do you have a family?'

The hammering stopped.

'What's that you say?'

'Do you have a family?'

'Yes!'

He gave the molten iron a tremendous blow. Irma went back to where Aurelian was waiting. It crossed her mind to give the blacksmith the money her father had given her but then she decided that that would be a stupid, capricious, affected thing to do. She remembered her father's stipulation: 'Something you really, truly want.' She compromised by telling herself that when she did eventually spend the money, she would bring a couple of hundred *lire* of the change to the singing Magyar blacksmith.

Then they went to the *lana di vetro* workshop, where they spin glass into women's tresses. It is a typical example of Italian playfulness, taking different materials and getting them to do the unexpected. In one of the old alleys there is a place where they weave iron chain links into curtains and drapes. In every corner *osteria* they put green pasta in your broth, grass-green because they use spinach to colour the dough. And four hundred years ago they used to spin fine sugar into napkins and tablecloths, so convincingly that the Emperor Heinrich once tried to wipe his hands on one at a banquet and watched in consternation as it splintered into pieces.

The *lana di vetro* was exceptionally beautiful. Irma saw how the glass was heated in a large cauldron. It looked just like sour cream and was transferred from there onto great wheels which were turned by a whey-faced girl, who spun it round and round until it was filament-thin and then let it unravel into supple, shimmering strands. It was so lovely; Irma felt that she 'had to have' some. She bought a bunch. It cost her two *lire*. The thousand *lire* note remained safe in her handbag.

Aurelian looked at his watch.

'Would you excuse me?' he said. 'My time's up. I've got to get back to the bank.'

'Already?'

'It's almost half past two.'

'It can't be. Have we really been together for an hour?'

'Yes. You got here at half past one.'

'How funny, it feels like ten minutes. Oh well—but at least let me walk there with you.' (I shouldn't have said that, she thought.)

'You're very kind.'

They went about twenty paces, then ducked under a *sottoportego*, and then suddenly there they were, in front of the bank.

'Already?'

'Yes, this is it. Thank you for coming with me. I'll say goodbye.'

Standing in front of the plate-glass doors, Aurelian shook her hand but made no mention of when they might see each other again. Not a single word.

With clumsily feigned insouciance, Irma said, 'When will I see you?' She felt the corners of her mouth twitch involuntarily. She was affecting a flippant society manner. She was acutely aware of how inappropriate she was being.

'Later this afternoon. I have an appointment with your father after six. He wants to me to take down some letters.'

At the relief of hearing this, Irma said lightly, 'Oh, after six? I might be at home then. Mother is unwell, you see. And then you'll get to see Judith at last.'

'Who is Judith?'

'Mothers nurse. When you came to see us the day before yesterday she had gone to the chemist's.'

'I see. And—will it be such an event for me, to see Judith at last?'

'She's prettier than I am. Older, but prettier.'

'What do you mean?'

'She's prettier because she works for a living. Work is invigorating, revitalising, I think. People who don't work get old and careworn, like me. The only time I really blossom is when I'm dressed up for the evening. Judith is much prettier than me in the daytime.'

Irma suddenly realised that she had not let go of Aurelian's hand. Perfunctorily she shook it, restoring the hand-grasp to its social function.

What a lot of nonsense I talk! she thought. What on earth must he think of me?

He went in through the plate-glass doors and she saw him disappear behind a counter, into the shadows. Slowly she made her way back past the shop window displays, stopping here and there, but her thoughts kept projecting themselves behind the glass; she scarcely saw all the goods that were being offered. She passed the two famous jewellers' shops. Then she remembered the thousand *lire* in her bag.

'No,' she said out loud, rebuffing the window display with a shake of her head. Jewellery was not her line.

A little later she found herself in front of an array of exquisite, expensive Burano lace, each piece as big as a bedsheet. That might be a possibility.

Next, she came to a much cheaper shop, little more than a bazaar, its window filled with stumpy little cigarette cases made of simple pressed leather. They had price tags on: five *lire*. They're not something to spend my thousand *lire* on, she thought, but I like them all the same. She went in and bought a very small one. As she handed over the money, she asked,

'Do you have any bigger ones? Suitable for a man?'

'Certainly.'

They brought one out. It held twenty cigarettes. Eight *lire*. She liked it. It was neat, useful, tasteful, original. Aurelian always smoked his Macedonias from a paper packet.

'Will you take this one too?'

She handed it back, suddenly ashamed of herself.

'Thank you, not this time.'

Somewhat flustered, she left the shop. She crossed St Mark's Square towards the waterfront. She was wearing a white dress and a white crochet-work hat with a little pompom on top. Two Italian officers in highly polished boots went past and one of them turned to look at her. Irma turned her head away and stopped, nervously waiting until the officers were some distance behind her. Then she went down to the quayside and stood at the water's edge, looking at the lagoon as it boiled in the sunshine. Behind her the Orologio clock chimed three. How empty the time was going to seem until six o'clock, she thought. Or possibly six thirty.

4

It was a quarter to seven. Irma was in her room, sitting in a corner of the sofa, reading. She put her book down when she heard Aurelian's voice through the open door. He was in the living-room, taking his leave of her father. Mr Lietzen was thanking him for typing so many letters. His voice was loud, warm, cheery. He was very grateful. Then suddenly, in the middle of a sentence, he stopped. There was complete silence for a moment. Then came Aurelian's voice:

'No, no—oh no! Thank you, but I couldn't. No, really.'

Irma snatched up her book at stared at it. The reason for the sudden silence was completely clear. She could perfectly reconstruct the dumbshow of her father shaking Aurelian's hand and pressing a banknote into his palm at the same time. Excruciating.

'No, truly, not for the world,' came Aurelian's voice again. 'It was nothing, really. I'm just glad that I could be of service.'

They said their goodbyes. Mr Lietzen was off to Milan for a few days.

Aurelian had almost left the living-room when Irma called out.

'Father!'

'What is it, my dear?'

He came and stood in the doorway. Aurelian stood beside him and bowed.

'Are you going out?'

'Yes, my dear. To the café.'

'All right. Have a good evening.'

Mr Lietzen went. Aurelian embarked on an apology.

'I didn't realise that you were here. Otherwise…' He made a gesture to indicate that had he known she was here, he would have come in to pay his respects. She was looking very pretty, he thought, with her thick fair hair silhouetted against the sunset, her eyes nervous and bright. 'Am I disturbing you?' he asked.

'Not in the slightest.'

He came into the room.

'Come and sit with me for a little.' She sat forward on the sofa, pulling her dress, which had got a little rucked up, back down over her knees. She had changed since that afternoon. She was now wearing a plum-coloured dress with white dots.

Aurelian began to make conversation.

'Your father is off on his travels again. What a restless life he leads!'

'Yes, poor dear. And it's all done for our sake, you know. Everything, absolutely everything. But at least he's started taking us with him when he goes on his travels. It's been like that for a year or two. He wants to show me the world before he dies, he says.'

'And how do you like the world?'

'Not a great deal. There are so many strangers in it. I prefer being at home—family, neighbours, friends. Such terrible things happen in the world and there's nothing I can do about any of it. At least at home we can all band together and help each other.' She felt herself close to tears. 'It's awful,' she said, 'just awful what goes on in the world. And I'm ashamed to say I don't fully understand all the stories I hear. I can't fight against any of it. I can't contribute anything. All I can do is be afraid. I envy those poor girls I saw in Vienna, marching along the Ringstrasse, arm in arm with about ten thousand others. They were angry, they were shouting... I've no idea what political party they belonged to. I'm sorry, I'm afraid I've started crying. I get like this sometimes. I'm a bundle of nerves.' She began fiddling with her book, turning her face away from Aurelian.

'What are you reading?'

She showed him. 'Pitigrilli[13]. In German. It's so honest, so brave! I think that's what's got me worked up like this.'

She stood up and went to look out of the open window, using it as an opportunity to dry her eyes. She stood there for a long time, saying nothing.

Aurelian went and stood beside her. 'You're doing it again. Looking very intently at something. I hope you won't take it amiss this time if I ask you what?'

Irma tried to smile. 'I'm looking at that ship. It's enormous.'

'It needs to be. It's going to South America.'

Irma let out a little sigh. Then she turned to face him. 'Let's go too! To South America! Shall we? Right now?'

Now it was Aurelian's turn to try to smile, but it wasn't a very successful attempt.

The lagoon was a blaze of colour. For as far as the eye could see, its waters were alight, those waters once dubbed the sacred defences of the Republic. Up in the sky, red and yellow streaks of light were blending into one as the sun sank to its rest. Its burning day's work was done and a beautiful drowsiness had set in. Far away in the distance, as far as the row of houses gleaming orange on the Lido, the lagoon began to glow, playfully mimicking the colours of the sky and of the sulphur-yellow, golden-fringed train of cloud which the sun slowly dragged down with it below the distant horizon.

When Aurelian spoke again, his voice was full of the superciliousness of the Venetian resident.

'It's so much more beautiful than the Danube, don't you think?' he said softly.

Irma was defensive. 'No, I don't.' Without looking at him she went on, 'And I'll thank you not to speak so slightingly of the Danube.' Her tone was somewhat haughty. 'Don't knock it like that. That's so typical of the way people behave when they go abroad. They start claiming that everything is so much better than back home. The Austrian Danube is just a hoax, if you ask me. The Viennese are forever calling it blue but that doesn't mean it is. Because in actual fact the real Danube isn't blue at all. The real Danube is my grey-brown Danube. That's the truly beautiful Danube. Around Tahi and Vác[14], upstream from the long island. All murky and bosky and riddled with sandbanks. Its like a great big, slow-moving, glassy lake. And the things I love most about it are the things which aren't in the least romantic. Chickens—vegetables—fruit floating down it. Market barges puttering along... They are always singing on those barges in the evenings. And all my friends... The old harbour masters, tanned like teak from the sun. Don't you dare go laughing at me. I've always thought that women love their country more than men do.' She stopped. 'Oh Lord, I don't know what's wrong with me today!'

'You're homesick.'

'No. It's not that.'

She raised her head to look at him, her eyes frank and open. Then a soft voice came from behind them.

'Excuse me, Irma...'

It was Judith.

'My mistress is asking for you.'

Irma's face was irresolute. 'She wants me right now?'

'Yes, I think so.'

'Very well, thank you. I'll be back shortly. And meanwhile, let me introduce you. Aurelian Szabó, this is Judith—do feel free to tell her what I said about her.'

Aurelian looked embarrassed. Irma's voice was so brittle

and forced. The three of them stood awkwardly in silence for a moment, then Irma went to her mother's room, leaving the living-room door open behind her.

Now it was just two of them standing awkwardly in silence. And then at last came a stock question that broke the ice:

'Do you live in Venice?'

'Yes,' Aurelian replied.

'And what do you do here?'

'I? Oh, nothing that fits any accepted model, I'm afraid. I mean, in Venice one should either be an Italian prince or an English lord, or a gondolier or a hotel porter, or a German tourist or an art historian or a honeymooner. One certainly shouldn't be a bank clerk.'

He had revealed more about himself in the space of a few seconds than over the course of three full days with Irma. As he looked politely at Judith, he was thinking about what Irma had said. 'She's prettier in the daytime.'

'I hope you don't expect me to feel sorry for you,' Judith said. 'I'm here as a nurse.'

They had both got off on the wrong foot, on a note of slight bitterness, and it made their conversation feel strained. And behind Judith's 'I'm here as a nurse' smouldered the dark, swooning, passionate eyes of the captive odalisque. Her voice, though, was matter-of-fact, almost prim.

'A nurse,' said Aurelian. 'Well, it's a blessed calling, after all. Akin to being a nun.' He looked at her eyes.

'That's true. But a nun... I wouldn't have the strength to be a nun.'

'Does it require strength? I would have thought that faith was enough.'

'It requires strength for a nun to renounce the thing she...' Judith broke off abruptly. Then, in rather a hard voice, she said, 'I am one of those women for whom the chance to have a child is extremely important.' Instinctively, without realising she was doing it, she turned her eyes to meet his.

Aurelian was a little taken aback by her forthright tone but he didn't show it. He tried to smooth things over.

'You should get married, then.'

But Judith would not be put back on the leash.

'That's not important. It's the child that matters.'

'Well, I mean, of course, yes, the child is important. But—I mean, please don't mind my asking, but—well, who will be the father?'

'Someone I'll adore.'

Silence greeted that remark. Aurelian felt uncomfortable.

'That won't be an easy person to find,' he said.

'I know.'

The metallic glare of the setting sun caught Judith's face. It isn't daytime any longer, Aurelian realised, but she's still prettier than Irma.

'On the other hand it would be easy to find someone who would...' He stopped. He was expressing himself clumsily.

'Someone for whom you'd be very…'

The slumbrous Ottoman eyes regarded him questioningly.

'I don't know what you mean.'

'I mean a—a conventional…' Once again he stopped, cursing himself for being so gauche. He smiled. Then Irma came back and he almost breathed a sigh of relief. 'I was just waiting for you, Miss Lietzen. I didn't want to go before properly taking my leave.'

'Where will you go now?' Irma asked. She saw Aurelian looking at her in astonishment. 'I beg your pardon,' she mumbled. 'Forget what I said.'

Aurelian took his leave.

Irma was standing with her back to Judith. Without turning round, she asked, 'How did you like him?'

'He seems pleasant. Was he Mr Lietzen's secretary?'

'Yes.'

Judith left the room, leaving Irma alone in the gathering dark. Her throat felt choked with tears. She had been like this all day, for no apparent reason. It was just a sort of restlessness which would no doubt disappear once she had had a good night's sleep. There had been a faint, insidious sirocco blowing for the last few days and it was fraying everyone's nerves. Nobody was sleeping properly.

The *Gazzetta di Venezia* was lying on the table. Irma picked it up and sat down with it, in the corner of the sofa once more. It annoyed her that it was always Aurelian who was saying goodbye. It was always he who had to hurry off somewhere. It was bad manners, quite frankly. That was the conclusion she came to as she flicked through the Italian newspaper. She turned to the last page, to the classified advertisements. These at least were interesting. She might find something for her thousand *lire*.

For heaven's sake just forget this Aurelian business, she told herself. Concentrate on yourself instead.

Judith came quietly back into the room.

'Reading an Italian newspaper?' she said, surprised.

'Just the classified ads. Darling Papa gave me a wad of money to buy something beautiful. I saw a lovely mirror I thought I might get. But I'm having a look here too, just in case...'

Judith went and stood by the window. Irma looked through the advertisements in silence. There was nothing much of interest among the cacophony of capital letters. There was 'Real Amber', advertised in English for the benefit of British tourists. There were the *Vetrerie*, the Murano glassworks. There was Burano lace. Murano, Burano. It reminded Irma of *Carlino-Berlino*. That was when Aurelian had been nicest to her. They had both been in a good mood that day. *Stoffe, Damaschi, Velluti*. Reproductions of old textiles... Those could wait until she had a home of her own, she thought. A lamp decorated with thirty-one different kinds of glass fruit. The glass wool factory—Aurelian hadn't been particularly nice to her there. *Frigidaire* (Yes, that just about summed it up). *Ferro battuto*, Venetian wrought-iron work (That reminded her, she wanted to give the Hungarian blacksmith two hundred *lire*—though the Hungarian blacksmith hadn't been particularly nice either, now that she came to think of it). *Antichità* (She could probably get a lovely mirror from them). Jesurum, the famous laces. And then, suddenly, in big letters: *T'amero sempre*! I will always love you. An advertisement for a cinema with the name of a film. *Mosaici*, glass mosaic, ready made or made to order. *Occasione*.

I don't want any of these things, she thought. I'd be wasting my money. Daddy has certainly made things difficult for me. *Lloyd Triestino*, *Terra Santa*. A trip to the Holy Land (Fine if one had someone to explain it all…). And then: Istituto Detectives…

What can that be about? *Istituto Detectives F. Prosper, autorizzato*. And an address underneath, and then two more lines: *Segrete informazioni private, matrimoniali, commerciali. Sorveglianze*. Interesting. *Segrete informazioni private*. Secret personal information. A private detective's agency. *Sorveglianze*. Surveillance…

Irma was no longer looking at the newspaper. Aurelian had never revealed the slightest personal thing about himself, she realised. Not once. Her eyes shone with a sudden bold idea. Her heart began to thud a little. Aurelian had a woman here, he must have. Was she a girlfriend, a mistress? Irma tore a little section out of the newspaper, the bit with the address of the detective's agency, tucked it into her bag and stood up.

Judith turned from the window. 'Did you find something?'

Affecting to sound offhand, Irma replied, 'Yes, I think so.' She looked at her watch. It was a quarter to eight.

'Something you really, truly want...' her father had said.

'I think I'll go out for a bit,' Irma said. 'I'll be back for dinner.'

She could barely move for the number of people who were strolling along the waterfront. Her heart was thudding harder now, she was possessed with an overpowering desire: now, at once! It's pointless what I'm doing, she thought. But so what? She was trying to reach St Mark's Square, from where she would be able to get her bearings. In her hand she clutched the little scrap of newsprint with the address of the detective's agency on it. Whenever a gap in the crowd appeared, she broke into a little run. I've got to be home for dinner, she told herself. Oh Heavens, I'll never find this place! St Mark's Square was thronged and she had to push her way through. At this time of day, when the Venetians have gone home to dinner and the pigeons have retired to roost, the Piazza is overrun with foreigners. Not only on the ground, above it as well. Groups of tourists amble across the flagstones; and above them, in the sky, there are groups of transient visitors of another kind: thousands of swallows, swooping wildly in thick flocks. English, German, Hungarian swallows... They are on their way home for the summer holidays...

Irma glanced up at them, then sighed, then stopped in front of a shop window to look at the address on the piece of paper by the light of the electric lamp: Rio Terrà Gregolini. And a number: 2871. She stopped a waiter outside Florian's, deliberately choosing an elderly one.

'*Prego, Rio Terrà Gregolini?*'

The waiter shook his head. She hurried on. She was in luck, a policeman was coming towards her.

'*Prego, Rio Terrà Gregolini?*'

The policeman pointed across the Piazza. 'Go under the *sottoportego* beside Caffè Quadri, then straight on, across two bridges until you come to a small square—*Poi domandi.*'

It is a curious and clever habit the Venetians have, this *Poi domandi*, 'Then ask again'. Everyone from waiters to policemen, porters to shop assistants, uses it as a way of giving directions to foreigners who are searching for a particular street or church. A policeman in Berlin would say, 'Take the second street on your left then the fourth on your right, then go diagonally right across the square and right again at the sixth turning and then you'll see it on your left,' but the inquirer gets lost halfway through the explanation and muddles everything up. Here in Venice people give directions for part of the way and—*Poi domandi*. Find someone else and ask again.

Irma ran on and asked again. Her route took her across bridges, beside canals, across squares, under tunnels beneath buildings and down alleys so narrow that two people could not have squeezed past each other…*Poi domandi*! On and on she went, over more little bridges spanning dank, malodorous waters, meeting fewer and fewer people, but she knew she was on the right track because the last person she asked didn't say '*Poi domandi*' but '*Ecco!*' Rio Terrà Gregolini opened out behind a black church squeezed behind a row of houses. Cats darted past the dark façades as Irma, panting slightly, came to a standstill in front of a small door. Above it was written the magic number: 2871. And beside one of the seven bell pulls on the wall was a small brass name-plate: Flaminio Prosper.

Irma tugged on the bell.

How on earth will I find my way back to the hotel? she wondered. She went up the narrow wooden stairs.

Flaminio Prosper was sitting in the kitchen in his shirtsleeves, with his wife. He was asthmatic and tremendously fat. He looked more like a butcher than a private detective. He spoke a bit of broken French so that somehow, half in French and half in Italian, he and Irma managed to communicate. He apologised for not being in his office. It was on the ground floor but he closed at six. He noticed that Irma was staring in something like alarm at his massive belly and thick neck. It seemed that he was used to people finding his appearance alarming for he said at once that there was no need to worry, he did not conduct any of his investigations himself, he had very able people to do that. The little soot-scented kitchen was suddenly filled with the story of his professional tragedy. Flaminio Prosper had been the best private detective in Venice but had had to give it up because his illness made him so fat that people literally stopped to stare at him in the streets. Under such circumstances, when one's outward appearance becomes so disastrously noticeable, it is obviously impossible to carry out any kind of under-cover operation, secretly tailing someone or walking up and down for hours outside a particular building. But Mr Prosper was still in charge of the agency and Irma could be absolutely assured of his discretion. So: it was a gentleman's movements that she wished his people to track?

'Yes.'

'Your husband?'

'No. My—my fiancé.' She almost burst into tears. She felt that she was up to her neck in quicksand.

'Track his movements,' said Prosper, reaching for a slip of paper.

'Yes.'

'Please come into the living-room.'

'No—oh no! I'm in the most fearful hurry and—and no one knows where I've gone. It's a secret…'

'Of course it is. Calm yourself, Miss. Please, take a seat. We'll take care of everything, don't you worry. Don't get yourself worked up, just wait until we send our report. Won't you sit down?'

'No.'

'The name of the gentleman in question?'

She spelled it out for him. '*Dottore*... Aurelio... Szabó. S, Z, A, B, Ó.

It brought the blood to her cheeks to hear her own voice speaking his name like that.

'His address?'

'Pensione Corti. He works as a bank clerk.'

'Don't work yourself up so, Miss. You'll soon see that there's not a word of truth in any of it.'

Irma looked startled. 'Any of it? Any of what?'

'Well, I mean to say, you clearly didn't come here for no reason. I expect you've heard some sort of rumour.'

'N—no,' she stammered, 'not a rumour...I just want to know...whether he...'

She twisted and crumpled her little bag as she spoke. Prosper looked at her with something like real affection.

'You'll see, Miss, there's nothing at all to worry about. That's how it'll all turn out. Don't get yourself into a state. I'm an honest man and I enjoy taking on cases which restore a person's peace of mind.

In the dark Rio Terrà, in the evil smelling, tumbledown house, in the grimy kitchen, those words coming from that lumbering, sick monster of a man, sounded so good and pure. It was enough to bring tears to Irma's eyes. She was a bundle of nerves, she couldn't sleep, she was so sensitive, so touchy, so tired. And now she had gone and done this thing, because she hadn't been able to stop herself.

'A deposit. Of course.'

She gave him the thousand *lire*.

('Something you really, truly want…')

'And your name?'

'It's not important.'

'Well, of course, but—to whom should I send my report?'

'Oh no, good Lord, you mustn't *send* it! No, no. I'll come back for it. I'll come for it myself in a day or two.'

Back she went down the stairs. She took a long, hard look at the little door so that she would know it again in the daytime. Then she hurried back down the Rio Terrà.

I don't care, I don't care, I don't care! He *must* have a woman. He *can't* not have a woman. I'm *sure* he has a woman…

And suddenly she felt completely calm. Suddenly she knew what was wrong with her. Something she hadn't wanted to admit before but which now was blindingly obvious.

5

Saturday, Sunday, Monday. Three days. Might Flaminio Prosper have some news by now?

No, it was too soon.

Tuesday, Wednesday. Five days. Irma went back to the Rio Terrà. She almost found her way there without asking anyone. A route associated with unhappiness sticks in the mind more clearly than one where the memories are serene.

But as soon as she saw the little doorway she turned and hurried away again. It wasn't just apprehension that made her do it. It was because, now that the time had come to face the painful truth, she needed to muster as much self possession as possible...

'I see. I'll come for it tomorrow, then, without fail.'

At six o'clock, Aurelian came to their hotel. Mr Lietzen was in Milan so Aurelian was taking the ladies out. The plan had been for them all to go for a bite to eat in St Mark's Square. But then, at the last minute, Mrs Lietzen announced that she was staying in. The young people should go by themselves. Irma was not particularly disappointed. In fact, she felt a surge of unexpected pleasure. She had *carte blanche* to wander about with Aurelian from six o'clock in the evening until late into the night. It is a very delightful feeling to be handed such a large amount of time like that, as an unanticipated gift.

But it never does to rejoice too soon. Her happiness was quickly dashed to pieces.

'Judith, you must go too,' averred the white-haired matron. 'You're spending all your time cooped up indoors with me. You're not getting a chance to see anything of Venice.'

All at once Irma understood why her mother was not going with them. If she was sending everyone away like this, it could only mean one thing: it was hair-washing night. The silver-haired Mrs Lietzen imagined it was a secret. She had no idea that her husband and daughter had long known all about it. At times like this, when she had the bathroom entirely to herself, she set about washing her hair with common-or-garden laundry bleach, to stop it from turning yellow. She treated her hair exactly like a laundress treats a fine white shirtfront. She had learned the trick from a Parisian actress who was famous for her luxuriant snowy locks and she made sure to keep it a secret for fear of other people hearing about it and starting to do the same thing.

Judith made no objection. She fetched her hat and bag and went with them.

I shan't address a single word to her all evening, Irma told herself as she rattled down with them in the lift. In the lobby, in the two leather armchairs, Fred and Bunny were already—or still—fast asleep, hand in hand. Bunny was pinker and plumper than when she arrived. Fred seemed to be getting even younger. His school-leaver's face had rounded down into that of a boy in the Lower Sixth. They were head over heels in love with each other. They had eyes for no one and nothing else.

'How pretty Bunny is,' whispered Judith as they tiptoed past them.

Irma didn't spare their slumbers. 'Fred is prettier,' she said loudly.

Fred woke up, grinned at them, and fell back to sleep again.

Irma did not really think that Fred was better looking. She just said it because Judith had complimented Bunny, and the reason she had spoken so loudly was purely because Judith had whispered. She was annoyed with Judith. It had been pushy and forward of her to come out with them that evening.

They walked along under the arcades of St Mark's Square. Rather too pointedly, Irma kept her eyes fixed on the window displays. Looking at shop windows is a good excuse for staying silent when one does not feel like talking. She soon got bored, though.

'Nothing but glass beads,' she said crossly.

They had seen so many coloured glass beads by now. One shop after another after another, so that their eyes were practically swimming. Great skeins of them, in every colour of the rainbow, hung like waterfalls in all the shops, sprouted like tendrils from the doorposts, shone in great heaps on the counters. All along the waterfront, bead hawkers had ropes of them dangling from their wrists. Stout saleswomen set up bead stalls and shrilly touted their wares. As flowers are to Nice, so coloured glass beads are to Venice, a perpetual, riotous surfeit of clashing colours, one of the sources of the Republic's medieval prosperity.

Judith bought a cheap string of beads the colour of Burgundy wine.

'What do you think?'

Irma shrugged. 'It's all right as a present for a little girl, I suppose.'

'I didn't get it with that in mind,' said Judith. 'I bought it for myself.'

And she fastened it around her lovely white neck.

They found a space to sit down outside Caffè Lavena. The Piazza was crowded and the orchestras were squealing in each of the four corners. All old Venice hands have attempted this and all have come to the same conclusion: it is impossible to find a place where you aren't bombarded by at least two orchestras at once. Judith pulled a mock-grimace as first from the left, then from the right, her ears were assailed by different melodies.

Serves her right, thought Irma (there are times when we all regress to the moral level of a five-year-old). That's what she gets for butting in on us.

Aurelian was sitting between the two girls but leaning towards Judith, replying to a question she had just asked.

Irma seized his arm. 'There's something I've been wondering,' she said. 'What's a *Rio Terrà*?'

'I'll tell you in just a minute,' said Aurelian. He turned back to finish what he had been saying to Judith about the four bronze Horses on the Basilica façade.

'…Napoleon had all four of them taken to Paris but later the French gave them back to Venice. Napoleon stole the big winged Lion on top of the column, too, and that was given back as well.'

'That's not fair!' pouted Irma. 'Between the bit about the four Horses and the bit about the Lion there was a natural gap. You could have answered my *Rio Terrà* question then. The thing about the Lion could perfectly well have come after the *Rio Terrà*.'

But Judith didn't agree.

'Sorry to be pedantic but no, the two things were linked. The main point of the story was neither the Lion nor the Horsesl; it was Napoleon, who made off with all of them.'

'And now, Miss Irma,' said Aurelian genially, 'you have my undivided attention and I'll tell you what a *Rio Terrà* is. It's a street which was once a canal but which has been filled in. And just so you realise what a decent fellow I am, to have broken off to answer your question now, let me point out that I did so even though the Napoleon topic was still not quite exhausted. Because what I wanted to add was that the St

Mark's Square we see today is in fact a product of Napoleon's genius because he closed it on the fourth side with that big *palazzo* over there.' He pointed to the Procuratie Nuovissime building at the far end.

Irma looked defiantly in the opposite direction, at the Basilica. There were people wandering about on its roof. Thirty or forty tourists, a mixture of ladies and gentlemen, scattered among the white saints and the golden angels like flies on an iced gâteau. There was another posse of tourists on the balcony of the Orologio, milling around the figures who strike the bell; and on top of the Campanile there was an even giddier group, peering down from the bell-chamber. It is an everlasting, primeval human instinct. The knowledge that 'It's possible to go up it…' leads on to 'Well, since we're here, we might as well…' Intensely irritating for those on the ground. Forwardness, that's what it was, Irma thought. Pushiness. Cheek. Just like Judith, she almost said out loud.

Judith and Aurelian were talking together quietly.

'What sort of view do you have from your window?' Judith wanted to know.

'Oh, a higgledy-piggledy jumble of tiled roofs and chimney stacks. But it's a nice view because the houses are all quite small and low. Their rooflines are a good way below my window, which gives me a big patch of sky and a view of the Campanile and the five tallest iron crosses on top of St Mark's.'

'Do you spend a lot of time looking out of the window?'

'Yes, in the evenings, when I'm feeling gloomy.'

'Do you often feel gloomy?'

'Quite often.'

'Do you write a lot of letters?'

'Not many. Long ones, though, when I do write.'

'I'm the same.'

Interesting, thought Irma. He tells her everything. Such personal things, too. And what a detailed description he gave of the view from his window. Painting a picture of himself in such deep, sentimental colours.

Judith was asking another question.

'Do you like reading?'

'Very much. I read a good deal.'

'Do you know D.H. Lawrence?'

'No.'

'Oh, then you have a treat in store! I've just finished *The White Peacock*. I can lend it to you if you like.'

'That's very kind of you, thank you. It's good to immerse oneself in a novel when one's a long way from home. If I'm enjoying a book I'll often go straight back home to it after work. I've been known to go to bed at eight o'clock and just read.'

'Why have you never told *me* any of this I'd like to know?' said Irma.

'I didn't imagine it would interest you.'

'And you *do* imagine it would interest Judith, is that it?'

That had been a bit too snappy, she realised.

'I don't know,' Aurelian said.

The Ottoman eyes were looking upwards, at a cloud above their heads.

Aurelian tried to defend himself. 'Judith asks better questions than you.'

Asks better questions? It was not much of a compliment. But even so, in her five-year-old mood, Irma could not bear the idea of Judith doing anything 'better', no matter how trivial or mundane. And what cheek on Aurelian's part, to present the whole thing as if she were somehow in competition with Judith. Who did he think he was? And Judith was just sitting there, maintaining a pained martyr's silence. I'm the fool, Irma thought, for staying here and putting up with them.

A constant stream of passers-by came and went in front of them. Their table was placed quite a way out into the square; they were sitting in the row furthest from the café itself, and they made a picturesque sight: a good-looking, dark-haired man between two attractive women. A lot of people turned to look at them.

I bet one of them is Flaminio Prosper's man, Irma thought. Which one is he, I wonder? She tried to guess which of all the many people who went past them was the detective. Tomorrow without fail she would go and pick up the report. The past half-hour had been the worst she had spent since coming to Venice. She had had enough. What was the point of sitting here any longer, feeling more and more annoyed?

'Let's go,' she said. She stood up.

Deferentially, a little too rapidly, Judith did the same. With that one hurried gesture, she made their relative positions as 'Daughter of the House' and 'Nurse' seem very pronounced. Their eyes met. Those of the highly strung young girl and the slumbrous odalisque. There was a flame burning in each but in Judith's gaze it was the steady, banked-down fire of something burning which was meant to be burning; coal in a grate, for example. What flickered in Irma's eyes was something wild and against the law, the blaze of something burning that shouldn't be, as if the drawing-room window curtains had been set on fire.

They made their way out of the square.

'Is this your bank?' Judith asked.

'Yes. It was clever of you to pick it out from among all the shops.'

'I looked at all the banks. There are several in the square. But yours is the one my eye alighted on.'

Sly flatterer! Irma thought. I might as well just take myself off home.

Judith was still talking to Aurelian. 'Don't forget that we're going bathing on the Lido on Saturday. That's right isn't it, Irma?'

'Yes. First thing in the morning.'

'In the morning?' Judith's voice was a little doubtful. 'Oh, but then Aurelian won't be able to come. He doesn't get off until the afternoon.'

Irma hadn't thought of that. She smiled bitterly. It had definitely been a mistake to let Judith come out with them. She's more considerate than I am, she thought. More selfless, more loyal—and more beautiful.

'I'm sorry,' she said, 'I quite forgot. All right, let's go in the afternoon. How lucky we are that Judith thinks of everything.'

Judith looked at Aurelian. 'A working person is always mindful of the constraints placed on a fellow worker.'

'How true,' said Aurelian.

They had stopped in front of a jeweller's shop in one of the little side streets. In the window was a notice: *Occasione*[15]. And beneath it, in a yellow velvet box, a bracelet. Six emeralds set in a wide band of diamonds. A hundred and ninety-five thousand *lire*.

'That's quite something,' said Aurelian. He turned to Judith. 'Are you fond of jewellery?'

Judith smiled and sighed. 'I adore it. It's the only luxury that interests me. I love precious stones.'

'I can't stand them,' Irma said. 'Come on.'

They went on their way. No one was enjoying themselves by now. They continued in silence towards the hotel. The worst of it is, thought Irma, that it isn't Judith who's not wanted here. It's me.

'Well,' Judith said after a while, her voice a little stiff, 'I thought that bracelet was gorgeous.'

Irma was seized with a sudden urge to make Judith suffer. Her instincts were those of a nasty little child. She turned to Aurelian with a sarcastic smirk.

'Why don't you buy it for her?'

Aurelian tried to laugh off the insensitive joke. 'One fine day, when I have the money!'

'And when that day comes, will you buy it for her then?'

'I hope so!' said Judith, laughing.

'For us, you know, poor as we are...' began Aurelian, his tone a little wistful.

But Irma was having none of it. 'Oh for heaven's sake!' she burst out, 'stop harping on about how hard-up you are!' She came to a halt on a little stone bridge and turned away from them, leaning on the chipped marble parapet and staring down at the water, unable to contain a sudden rush of tears. Down by the bank a gondolier was polishing the metalwork on his gondola, like a housemaid polishing door knobs. He looked up into the pretty face above him and called out.

'Gondola? Gondola?'

Irma's tears splashed into the canal. They were flaying her alive with all this talk of poverty. It was the second time they'd done it. It was a cast-iron bond between them, something that kept her firmly beyond the pale. She felt like a child who has been told by the others that she mayn't join in the game. She positively envied them for both being poor.

Judith and Aurelian had come to a standstill behind

her and were now waiting, saying nothing because it was obvious that she was crying—she was doing nothing to hide it—and it was equally obvious that they knew full well why. Irma was sure that they were exchanging scornful looks.

They were not quite doing that, as it happened. Judith was standing with her head bent to the ground. Aurelian could not take his eyes off her. His expression grew very serious as he stared at the infinite calm of that pale, immobile face.

6

On Saturday morning, Irma went to see fat Mr Prosper. He received her in his office, a wheezing mass of blubber. The 'office' was smaller than the Lietzens' larder in Tahifalu. Fat Mr Prosper could barely turn round in it. It was too small for him; he had grown out of it, like one grows out of an old shirt. He reached for a file. Irma waited for him to say something reassuring. 'You see, I told you there wouldn't be anything to worry about.' But he didn't. He sat down at the desk, opposite Irma, and unfolded a sheet of paper.

'It's in Italian,' he said, in an official-sounding voice. All trace of his former friendliness had vanished. 'I'll translate it for you.'

And he proceeded to do so, in a mixture of French, Italian and German. The report was very thorough. It went into quite a lot of unnecessary detail.

'At half past six in the afternoon he drank a glass of white vermouth at Giacomuzzi's… After dinner he went to hear the music in the Piazzetta with two other people from the bank… On Wednesday evening he was sitting with two ladies outside Lavena….

So one of the passers-by *had* been a detective, Irma thought.

'Oh?'

'An attractive little blonde and a stunning brunette. The ladies…'

'Just a moment. Who did you say he was with?'

'Two ladies. An attractive little blonde and a stunning brunette.'

That hurt. She pointed at the document on the table. 'How exactly is that expressed in Italian?'

'One of them a *graziosa biondina*, the other a *bellissima bruna*.'

Prosper was not a detective for nothing. He knew straight away who the *graziosa biondina* was. He offered this in consolation:

'Don't read anything into it, *Signorina*. My man is an Italian. They prefer brunettes.'

That was painful for Irma, too.

'The ladies,' Mr Prosper went on, still wheezing, 'were Hungarian. One of them…'

Irma interrupted him again. 'All right, all right, I know. Carry on…'

'After that he saw them home. He parted from them in front of the hotel but did not leave. Instead he waited by the door. After ten minutes the stunning brunette came out and handed him a book. They spoke for a long time. Then the brunette went back into the hotel and *Dottore* Szabó went home.'

That was new. Irma had not known about that.

'Then what?' she asked.

'The following day, Thursday, at four in the afternoon, the gentleman in question came out of the Pensione Corti, where he lives, in the company of a lady. He helped to put the lady's travelling trunks onto a gondola. Then he got into the gondola, beside the lady, and went with her to the railway station. The lady had been staying in the same *pensione* for a month, in room number 9. Her name is Frau Lotte Welitsch. She lives in Vienna, is twenty-nine years old and is a—how shall I say it—a nice-looking woman.'

'How is that expressed in Italian?'

'*Carina.*'

'Go on.'

'At the station there were a lot of people waiting for the train and they did not speak to one another. The lady more than once raised her handkerchief to her eyes, in the manner of someone who is silently weeping. They parted with a simple shake of the hand. The lady got into the direct Vienna compartment, and remained by the window until the train began to move. They did not wave to each other. When the train had gone, *Dottore* Szabó seemed relieved. He set off back to town on foot. On the way, he went into the church of San Giacomo, where he stood for a few minutes in front of the altar, with his head bowed. Then he sat down at the Osteria Vida, next to the church, where he drank a small glass of Soave and spent a lot of time jotting in a notebook.'

'All right, and then what?'

'That's all. The report from yesterday only came in at noon today. Shall I continue to have him watched?'

'No.'

Prosper found her answer completely rational. The Viennese lady had left, after all. Irma sat with her elbows on the desk, staring out of the window. She sat there for a long time. The window looked out onto a dirty-red brick wall. A cage hung from the window opposite and in it sat a bird, in obstinate silence. Irma looked at it for some time. Then she stood up.

'How much do I owe you?'

'Nothing. You gave me a thousand *lire*. My bill came to fourteen *lire* more but we won't worry about that.'

Dear, darling Daddy, if you only knew what I'd done! Irma thought.

Prosper pushed the piece of paper towards her. 'The report, *Signorina*.'

'Thank you.'

The mass of blubber looked at her sadly, like a doctor who is 'very sorry he cannot give a more cheerful diagnosis.' Prosper was a good-hearted and humane man, much more so than one might have expected. Irma had the impression that he had let her off the fourteen *lire* because he too felt that the report had been a depressing one.

She took her leave. Once down in the street, she tore the document into little pieces and flung them into the water from the first bridge.

Would she ever forget the contents of that report?

In the afternoon, as agreed, Aurelian came to pick them up for the bathing trip to the Lido. He was not taking them to the public beach but to the sandy stretch in front of the Excelsior, to give the girls a taste of that rarefied, glittering, international world, so entirely detached from all other life on the Lido.

Irma was waiting on her own in the hotel lobby.

'What about Judith?' Aurelian asked.

'She'll join us later. She still has things to do. Mother is getting dressed up because Mrs Lineman is coming for her. She's finally going to be taken to meet Countess Morosini.'

From the Hotel Danieli they took the small, exclusive motor launch that goes non-stop to the Excelsior and back. Irma was wearing the dark blue short-sleeved top again but this time she had not matched it with a skirt. Instead she was wearing dark blue baggy sailor's trousers, without stockings. It was the perfect outfit for the Lido. No longer as daring as it once would have been, it is nevertheless a style that only really looks good on one girl in a hundred. On the *graziosa biondina* it looked sensational, and the *biondina* knew it. It made her look like a loose-limbed, somewhat girlish, fair-haired boy. When Aurelian took her arm to steady her as she boarded the boat, she boldly jumped over the gunwale. The expressions on the faces of the other passengers clearly showed that they admired both the boldness of the gesture and the girl who had made it.

'You can't do that in a skirt,' said Irma, once they were sitting side by side on the cushioned bench, squeezed together amongst all the other passengers.

With the aid of a boat hook, the launch was eased out of the narrow canal. Then the engine began to roar and they took off across the lagoon. Aurelian took the colourful scarf out of Irma's hand and wound it carefully round her neck. Irma looked at him. In spite of the detective's report she had just received, she was filled with a kind of bitter-sweet happiness, from the top of her head to the tips of her toes. To be here with him, pressed up against him in the fresh sea breeze, just the two of them, as the boat sped along... All thoughts of detective's reports, conjectures, conclusions, theories and calculations simply evaporated beside the realisation that Aurelian was there beside her, in earthly flesh and blood, and that the other passengers were crammed in so tightly that she and he were pressed together from shoulder to knee. She clutched the bag with her bathing things on her lap. Today, for the first time, she would be wearing her apple-green swimming costume. Today was the first time Aurelian would see her body. She felt happy and proud, expecting him to like what he saw. She felt something akin to what an innocent young bride might feel, who on her wedding night, after dinner, at last takes the lift upstairs with her groom, safe in the knowledge that ten minutes later, he will like what he sees very much. Brought up in complete innocence, and by nature entirely demure, Irma felt a painful yet sweet constriction in her chest at the thought of Aurelian seeing her as she stepped out of the bathing hut. She lowered her eyes. I'm horribly in love, she thought.

She looked up at the other passengers. At the far end of the boat, a good-looking young Italian officer touched his cap. Irma returned the greeting warmly and Aurelian asked,

'Who's that?'

'Nino,' Irma said.

She waited for him to ask who Nino was but the question didn't come. Aurelian was looking out across the water. He pointed to a *sandolo* which was being propelled by four strapping young men in purple jerseys. They were rowing standing up.

'Look,' he said, 'it's something unique in the world. Regatta boats where the rowers stand up. It's an ancient Venice tradition.'

'I met Nino at the hotel,' said Irma. 'I don't know what his real name is. I didn't catch it when he was introduced. It was during afternoon tea. It was me who christened him Nino.'

There was a short silence.

'It's a perfect day for a swim,' Aurelian said. 'The sun is lovely and hot.'

'Nino is frightfully good looking.'

'Yes, he is.'

'So classically Venetian. I'm always hearing from girls

in Budapest about this Italian officer or that Italian officer. When they come back from Abbazia[16] or Viareggio or Venice there's always a Nino or a Paolo or an Enrico, and they dance like this and they dance like that... Well, now I've got one too.'

Aurelian took her hand. Irma was delighted. She imagined that he was about to start lecturing her about Nino. But instead, still grasping her with one hand, Aurelian pointed with his other hand to the island they were just passing.

'San Lazzaro. That's where Lord Byron lived.'

'Is it?' said Irma, forcing herself to sound interested. And to herself she added, 'That's how I have to play it.'

They reached the Excelsior landing stage, with its blue and white striped mooring poles. On the quayside stood porters in bright white uniforms, their gold buttons gleaming in the sunshine. Irma and Aurelian made their way to the hotel through a long tunnel, beneath chandeliers that shone by day, amid palm trees and flowering plants. It felt like a honeymoon—perhaps more like the wedding itself. Up wide marble steps they went, to the marble-columned, gilded, church-like hall... The only thing missing was the organ. Irma stopped. She took Aurelian's arm and gazed up at the chandeliers, which seemed to her like temple lamps. I'm horribly in love, she thought again.

'It seems that Nino didn't come for the sea-bathing,' remarked Aurelian, nodding towards a group whom Nino had joined for a cup of coffee.

'What a pity,' said Irma, and walked past Nino so that he would touch his cap to her again. He did so.

Once in the bathing hut, it only took her a moment to get changed. But she did not come out straight away. She sat down on the little bench and lit a cigarette. It was better like this, better if Aurelian was waiting for her and then she could suddenly emerge, like a fairy apparition. But then she berated herself. How stupid I am, behaving like this! I've never been so stupid in my life! She was suddenly filled with impatience. She counted to sixty, five times out loud, as a way of killing five minutes. Then she pulled on her green bathing cap and, like a nymph emerging from her grotto, stepped out of the bathing hut, prepared to dazzle the world.

Aurelian was nowhere to be seen.

And suddenly she was surrounded by about two hundred other women, all of them in a state of undress that was similar to her own—or even more advanced—in bathing costumes of a hundred different hues, standing, sitting, running, reclining on the sand. At first glance each woman seemed more beautiful and more brazen than the next. The notion of modesty began to seem like an outmoded, hypocritical human construct which our modern, sporty, healthy age has simply brushed aside. Very few of these women would have given two hoots for Péter Pázmány's[17] Shakespearean theory of the divine origin of female modesty, according to which the body of a dead man floats face upwards in the water whereas that of a drowned woman always floats face down. The Lido was full of ladies very far from dead, all floating face upward and barely concealed by the limpid water. And blue-blooded damsels were sauntering on the strand, the triangle-shaped scraps of their bathing suits serving to decorate rather than cover their comely bodies, revealing every contour to within a fine hair's breadth of the point beyond which only a doctor can respectably be granted a passport. And they were outrageously beautiful— even from close up—so that when the Danube nymph, with all her vaunted vanity, broke suddenly upon them, she was immediately lost in the beauteous crowd, forced to accept the dispiriting truth that she was very far from being the only woman in the world.

And still Aurelian was nowhere to be seen.

Irma picked her way across the burning sand, down to the sea, holding up a hand to shade her eyes and gazing out across all the human heads that were dancing in the green water. From some way out an arm was waving in her direction and above the shouts of the bathers she heard her name.

'Irma! I-i-irma-a!'

It was Aurelian. He had gone in up to his neck and was now cupping his hands around his mouth, using this time-honoured, primitive form of megaphone to call out to her.

'Come on in! The water's glorious!'

And so saying he turned and began to swim out to sea. He moved vigorously, his head ploughing through the foaming waves. So much for the bride's beating heart as she showed herself to her groom! Instead of his wonderstruck, trembling, enraptured face she saw nothing but two arms, rising and falling one after the other in the billows, far away and getting ever further. Irma stumbled back up the sand, away from the water, and came to a standstill halfway up the beach. She felt bitterly ashamed. And not a single member of this merry, romping crowd had a worry or a care in the world. The best thing she could do was get dressed again and go home.

She stood there for some ten minutes, staring at the sparkling green sea, so much deeper and bolder and livelier than the sluggish blue lagoon. And then, suddenly, Aurelian was beside her, his hair slicked across his forehead. He was panting a little after his vigorous swim and his eyes were shining.

'Why don't you come in?'

He smiled and looked into her eyes. Just her eyes, that was all he looked at. He really had nothing else on his mind but the question of why Irma didn't go into the water.

It's not Nino who's the frightfully good-looking one, Irma wanted to say. It's you. But what she said instead was,

'I was just looking at all these interesting people. But I'm going into the water now.' And off she rushed, rather frantically, towards the sea.

Aurelian went after her. He caught her up just as she was starting back onto the sand with a cry of pain.

'Ow—the water's boiling hot!' she cried.

'Of course it is, the sun has been shining on it since dawn. You have to hurry through the hot bit to get to the cold. Like this, watch…'

And he plunged into the water with an almighty splash, only stopping when he got some way out, to the part where it was cool, where the water reached up to his chest.

'He's not in the slightest bit interested in me,' said Irma to herself, and hurled herself into the water like a crazed suicide, urging herself further and further on until she came to where Aurelian was standing. When she reached him, he flung himself into the waves and began rapidly swimming out to sea, towards Trieste, towards Constantinople, towards India. Irma swam after him, her well formed bronzed shoulders cutting through the green water with its crown of white spume. But she couldn't catch him up. 'He's leaving me again,' she panted. Tentatively she put a foot down. She could still just stand, on tiptoe, with the water reaching to her chin. Desperately she called out.

'Aurelian!'

The bobbing head turned round.

'What's the matter?'

I'm horribly in love with you! she almost replied. But in fact she made no answer at all, just slowly started towards the shore, dancing across the soft silt, her arms making wide swimming motions. As more and more of her supple, slender figure began to emerge from the water, she looked down with childish pride at the virginal swell of her breasts. In the light green swimming costume, now wet and clinging to her body, she imagined that she looked like an ancient Roman bronze. Not a tall, curvaceous, white marble goddess, nothing like that, that was Judith's department. She was completely out of the water now. She raised her arms and looked at herself from the side, from armpit to ankle. I'm a firm young bronze Roman athlete, she thought. But I never dreamed it would be like this. He doesn't want to spend a single minute alone with me. He's a brute and I'm pining away for love of him and all he does is swim. And any minute now Judith will be here and that will be the end of it.

She looked back at the water. Aurelian had come out. Male and glistening with water droplets, he smiled at her, his white teeth gleaming in his tanned face. Irma stopped to wait for him. Her throat was choked with tears again, just as it had been on Wednesday afternoon when she had stood on that bridge, weeping into the canal. He'll have to look at me now, she thought. She lifted her head, stood tense and erect, her left hand on her hip. Aurelian seemed refreshed and in a good mood after his swim. He did look at her, but once again no further than the eyes. It was a look of innocent friendship.

'What was the matter with you just now?'

'Nothing,' she said and started off up to where the sand was warm and dry. It flashed through her mind that she needed to be bolder, to do something to force him to look at her. She turned around, smiling at him with her head coquettishly cocked.

'It's a funny feeling, don't you think, wandering around naked with so many other people?'

'Yes, I suppose it is,' Aurelian laughed. 'I feel a bit incomplete dressed like this, I must admit. I miss having a pocket. I never know where to put my hands. A pocket is a place where one's hand can tuck itself away, like a bird on a roosting perch or in a bush…'

Irma realised she was going to have to be even more brazen.

'For us women,' she said, 'it's difficult to know how to walk like this—undraped. In normal circumstances, you see, a women doesn't walk with her legs but with her skirt. The legs are there, of course, but they're hidden. Their job is to make the skirt move with a certain rhythm. What you men call a woman's way of walking is in fact the motion of her skirts. But like this—well, one has to reveal what one's legs are doing and that feels peculiar. It's all wrong, somehow. Like an owl forced into the daylight. Both legs— and one of them is always trying to hide itself behind the other. Look—see what I mean…?'

'You have a fine gait, loose and unfettered,' said Aurelian. His voice was as unemotional as that of a sports coach.

'It's because I take a lot of exercise,' Irma said. In her despair she lay down on the sand. She was horribly ashamed of having paraded herself like that. She would have liked to box her own ears. She lay on her back, her face in the sun, to make it turn brown and hide her embarrassment. She could feel that she was blushing.

Aurelian turned and hurried away.

'Where are you off to now?'

'To get you some dark glasses. Against the sun.'

'I don't need any!' she called after him, but he waved her words away and hurried off towards his bathing hut.

He was always running away from her. He'd done it again. A fat, glistening, one-and-a-half-carat tear trickled out from under her closed lids. I seem to cry at the drop of a hat these days, she thought. It's not normal. Still with her eyes closed, she smiled. He's bringing me a pair of sunglasses. He doesn't even want to look at my eyes now. She decided that it didn't matter that she was crying. Her face was wet from the sea in any case. He would never notice.

Aurelian handed her the sunglasses. She put them on without saying a word. She was lying stretched out on the sand, her arms held out at either side, like a cross. Aurelian sat beside her, his knees bent, his arms hugging his shins. They let the hot sun dry their bodies. From behind the protection of the dark glasses, Irma plucked at topics of conversation, prompted by some of the things that had been in the detective's report.

'What is the church of San Giacomo like?'

'It's an old church. Nothing special.'

'Have you been inside it?'

'Yes. It's got a very fine carved pulpit.'

'Close by, so I've heard, there's an *osteria* called Vida.'

'There is.'

'I'd like to go and eat there one evening. Whereabouts is it?'

'Not far from the railway station.'

Under the green swimsuit, her heart began to thud slightly. Aurelian had taken the bait so easily. As casually as anything, she went on,

'Have you been to the railway station recently?'

'Yes.'

The green swimsuit quivered a little. 'On Thursday.'

'Yes. I went to see a friend off.'

'A friend who was going to Vienna.'

'Yes. How did you know?'

'I just did. It was a woman.' The green swimsuit didn't quiver this time. It lay stiff as Irma waited.

'Yes.'

Irma breathed out and the green swimsuit came to life again. There was a long silence. Then Irma said softly,

'Tell me about it.'

'I don't like to talk about that sort of thing.'

'All right. Then tell me just one thing. Is—is it all over between you and the Viennese lady?'

'I'm sorry, I don't know what right you have…'

Clearly and distinctly she blurted it out:

'Because I'm in love with you.'

She lay completely still except for her two heels, which

117

dug deeper and deeper grooves in the sand, first one and then the other, right down to the point where the sand began to get cool and damp. Her eyes were tight shut. She felt as if her whole soul was taking refuge now behind the dark glasses. They sat in complete silence. All around them, people were laughing and shouting. The cheerful sound of people playing ball rose up from the water. The whole twenty years of her life so far had been leading up to this moment, Irma thought. In saying what she just said, she had emerged into adulthood. The time for childish play was over. Life had begun.

She sat up, then got to her feet. Aurelian got up too and stationed himself stiffly by her side, like a corporal beside his sergeant. As if ready to give an account of himself, he stood looking intently into her face. Irma's legs were noticeably trembling. She took off the dark glasses and smiled crookedly, twitching one corner of her mouth.

'Please take me to my bathing hut,' she said.

'I—what do you mean?'

'I mean carry me—*lug* me, like that time by the Danube.'

'What...?'

'I'll pretend I can't walk. That I've hurt my leg.' She laughed. Her face was drained of all colour.

'Look, I—I mean...'

Irma started walking, took two limping steps, then cried out in mock pain.

'Ow! My foot!' She laughed a frozen little laugh at the boy who was standing there stock still. 'Coward!'

Aurelian picked her up and set off with her towards the bathing huts. No one took any notice of them. No one so much as turned a hair. Irma looked up at him from where she hung, cradled in his arms.

'It's because of you that I love the Danube the way I do.' Her tears were falling freely now. 'The Danube—it's all because of you…'

Only a short while ago she had been in agony because Aurelian wouldn't look at her with anything approaching warmth. Now she was in his arms, tightly pressed against his body, but her proximity was having no effect on him. He was a million miles from having any tender thoughts towards her. A cold, clear feeling of unequivocal pain washed over her and she closed her eyes. This man did not love her and never would. This man loved Judith.

Back at the bathing huts, when Aurelian put her down and when she had taken a couple of deep breaths in an attempt to restore her composure, Irma saw Judith approaching through the crowd. She said nothing, pretending not to have noticed her. Judith went into a bathing hut to get changed.

I can't bear it, Irma said to herself, I'm going to run away.

And yet she did not have the courage to leave the two of them alone together. She stood leaning against her bathing hut for support, waiting for the blood to return to her cheeks. Aurelian waited beside her, his head hanging in an attitude of guilt. He did not speak. This lasted until Judith found them. She went up to them cheerfully, suspecting and noticing nothing. She was wearing a black bathing costume. Her pale skin made her look like a marble goddess. She was not plump but her figure was too rounded to be called sylph-like. Irma only looked at her for a brief second; her attention was immediately fixed by Aurelian's eyes. One should not try to explain these things; indeed one cannot. But it was fully evident that Aurelian was entranced by the sight of this beautiful, pale-skinned, womanly young girl. Irma turned back to look at Judith again. Her pallor was extremely beautiful. Beside her, Irma felt that the deep coppery suntan she had been so proud of was suddenly ridiculous. Why had she fried herself like that? It was all wrong. Her skin could be even whiter than Judith's if she wanted.

'You're beautiful,' she told Judith truthfully, loudly enough so that Aurelian could hear, succumbing to a woman's inherent urge to make herself suffer.

'What nonsense!' laughed Judith, abashed, and ran off into the sea.

It was a relief to Irma when all that candid marble beauty was immersed up to its neck in water, hidden from view. She felt disorientated, thrown off balance. Her thoughts darted wildly to and fro, her head was filled with rash ideas, demented plans for recourses to violence or a melodramatic renunciation of her dreams. Then each idea vanished as quickly as it had come. But like the pyrotechnician's torch at a fireworks display, when all the smoke and sparks have dispersed, there was one thought that persisted amidst the ephemera. It was something from a folk tale her father had once told her, about a proud princess who saw a beautiful peasant girl bathing in a stream and was filled with despair that God should have created such an exquisite creature alongside her, the high-born noble lady. When she got home, she undressed and stood weeping in front of her looking-glass. Then she summoned the court gilder and had her breasts covered in gold, after which she slept peacefully.

Judith emerged from the water and stood scanning the beach for them. The beautiful peasant girl looked more exquisite than ever. Aurelian stood staring at her, with one hand shading his eyes against the sun.

'We're over here!' he called, raising an arm aloft.

Judith came running towards them, stumbling a little in the deep sand. She came to a halt, panting, her hand pressed against her heart. Her face was decked in a bright smile, but beneath her snowy brow the swooning Ottoman eyes were like glowing coals.

'Don't keep staring at me like that!' she laughed at them, and quickly folded her arms to cover her chest.

Irma could bear it no longer. She went into her bathing hut, got dressed, then waited until the others had moved away before creeping out, making sure the coast was clear and then giving them the slip.

Judith and Aurelian took the Excelsior motor launch back to Venice at seven o'clock that evening, happy and refreshed after their swim. Among the crowd of passengers waiting for the launch on the long wooden jetty that stretches into the bay was Nino. By the time it was Judith's turn to get on, he was already aboard and he held out both his hands to her with a smile. Judith took one, and once safely on deck, thanked him politely for his help, smiling into his eyes in a way that does not come naturally to all women and which for Judith was something completely new.

'Do you find him good-looking?' asked Aurelian, glancing towards the officer as they sat down.

'Very,' said Judith. 'But just as a phenomenon, if you know what I mean.'

The 'phenomenon' deliberately chose a seat on the bench directly opposite Judith. The motor launch set off with a great roar. Both Aurelian and Judith felt pangs of conscience at Irma's disappearance. It was impossible to misinterpret it; they both knew full well why she had run away. They understood it instinctively, with the clear sight of a child or of a person in love. It was not even worth going into the psychological reasons. But somehow Judith felt compelled to talk about it. This was a new triumph for her and it was partly uncomfortable but partly rather delicious. She wanted to savour it a little, to bring the subject up just to see what Aurelian would say, in case he said something to make these few moments more delicious still. Aurelian looked at Nino in his highly polished boots. He was talking to the person sitting next to him.

'Everyone finds him good-looking,' he muttered to Judith.

'How strange Irma is,' said Judith. 'Just disappearing like that.'

There was a short pause and then Aurelian said,

'Regular features, very attractive, there's no denying it.'

'Who, Irma?'

'No. That officer. Do you know him?'

Judith did not reply. She narrowed her eyes, trying to think.

'What I'm racking my brains to remember,' she mused, 'is what we said after Irma went into her bathing hut. Because it seems clear that she got upset about something.'

'Do you think it was something I said?' asked Aurelian imperturbably.

'I don't see why it should have been. Do you think it was me?'

They were keeping up an entirely spurious conversation. None of it had anything to do with Irma's feelings. Judith was trying to tease out of Aurelian the words she wanted to hear and Aurelian was defending himself with words he didn't mean. And added to all of that, the officer opposite them was a genuinely fine figure of a man.

'Where did you meet him?' Aurelian wanted to know.

'At the hotel.'

And then she went back to her theme, like a cat falling back on its feet. 'I met him with Irma,' she said. And then,

'Irma's sweet. But such a typical little rich girl. It never occurs to her that other people have things to worry about, that they have their own lives.'

'She's very young,' Aurelian said. 'I find her charming. What with everything I've been through over the last terrible few days, it's been a pleasure to have her with me, chattering and laughing and skipping about.'

'It doesn't show,' said Judith. 'That you've been through a terrible few days, I mean.'

'Well, I don't usually let these things show. You've been very kind to me today. So patient and understanding, listening to my sorry story.'

'It was pure selfishness, I'm afraid. I wanted to know about—about your personal life.'

'Why?' He looked at Judith, his eyes greedy for her answer.

The Ottoman eyes did what so many pairs of eyes have done before at times like this: stared straight at the floor, then up to meet his, then down again. There was no need for more. More would have diminished the effect. Judith looked up from her feet and there, a little further away on the opposite bench, she saw the English honeymooners.

'Look! Fred and Bunny.'

This time it was only Fred who was asleep, his head lolling on Bunny's shoulder. Bunny was staring out with her big child's eyes at all the poles and marker posts that punctuate the lagoon. Fred was dressed from head to toe in white, with the exception of a bright scarlet cardinal's cap. Within a minute or two, Bunny had closed her eyes as well. Nino saw that Judith was looking at them. He edged forward on the bench, leaned towards Judith and said, above the din of the engine,

'*Ils dorment toujours, toujours!*'

They exchanged a few more words in French. Judith turned to Aurelian and asked, in Hungarian,

'Shall I introduce you?'

'No.'

'But it'll make me look rude.'

'Still, I'd rather you didn't.'

Judith shook her head disapprovingly.

'I mean, what's the point?' Aurelian went on. 'You don't speak Italian and I don't speak French. So how will we— you know...?'

'All right, all right, I won't introduce you.' And she turned brightly towards the handsome officer, asking him a question in French. Nino's reply made her burst out laughing.

Some distance away, far out in the lagoon, stood a fisherman with his trousers rolled up, the water coming up to his knees. Everybody turned to look at him. Beyond, far off on the distant horizon, was a scattering of about ten brick-red sails. It was as if the little skiffs had been set alight by the setting sun.

Judith looked at her watch and asked Nino another question in French. His response was very grave.

'*Non. Jamais.*'

Aurelian had no idea what they were talking about and did not ask. Only much later did he say, 'Are you keen on that fellow?'

'Oh, come now!'

'I only ask because you…'

'Very well then,' said Judith, a little more primly than was necessary, 'just to please you, I shan't look at him again. Not once. Not the single teeniest glance. Are you satisfied?'

But Aurelian had found another object for his ire. A tall, Spanish-looking man with glossy dark hair and beige-coloured trousers, who was now looking impudently at Judith. Aurelian knew him by sight. He had a reputation for taking girls out for a spin in his sports car and then getting them to pay for the petrol at one of the filling stations on the mainland. You're wasting your time with this particular girl, he thought. *She* won't be buying you any petrol.

As the big motor launch juddered along, it seemed to Aurelian that everyone was looking at Judith. It made him feel self-conscious.

'What an impression you're making,' he remarked.

Judith said nothing.

'I expect you must be used to it by now,' he went on, with an awkward smile. 'But I'm certainly not. It's the first time I've been with you in any kind of company and everybody is staring at you.'

The Ottoman eyes were turned on him gravely.

'Everybody except you.'

Looking straight ahead, with a rather sour smile, Aurelian said, 'Everybody except me. Excellent.'

When they got back to the Danieli, he made a great show of helping Judith onto the quay because he saw that Nino was about to offer to do so. Nino raised his hand to them and went on his way. Beneath his narrow moustache his lips twitched somewhat dismissively, the expression of a man who knows that another man finds him in the way and who demolishes his aggrieved rival's sense of victory with a smile of condescending sympathy: 'She's yours, be my guest, it's no skin off my nose. I'm leaving you to it, I'm off!'

Once back at the hotel they asked the concierge for Miss Lietzen.

'She's upstairs in her room.'

Judith held out her hand. Aurelian took it and did not let it go. He had not felt like this for a long time.

'Don't go up just yet. Please…'

They went back outside. Without exchanging a word they headed down to the water, turning in the opposite direction from the inevitable evening throng and noise and commotion. At the edge of the quay stood a gaggle of people, all looking admiringly at something. Aurelian and Judith went see what was going on. There on the water, nudging up against the quayside, bobbed a beautiful big motorboat with an enormous shiny brass dolphin on the bow and a bright white sun awning. All the fittings were of gleaming mahogany and copper and brass. A handsome young British naval officer was on board, and standing on the quay was another one, holding a boat hook.

'They're English...'

Three passengers arrived. Bare-headed, bespectacled young schoolteachers, simply clad in loose shirts and unfashionable, too-short trousers, fresh from playing tennis on the Lido, racquets in hand. Strapped onto each of their racquets was a pair of tennis shoes. They hurried past. The sailor with the boot hook elbowed a few of the onlookers aside, making way, then drew himself erect, tensing his neck in a salute. The three little teachers jumped nimbly aboard. The sailor then stepped down onto the bow and used the boat hook to ease the boat away from the quay. At the same moment, the engine snorted into life and all of a sudden the boat was gone. All that was left was its shiny brass dolphin, bounding straight as an arrow for the British battleship.

Nino—(where on earth had he sprung from?)—leaned across to Judith confidentially.

'British naval officers, would you believe?'

Aurelian looked at him, then looked away again.

'One of these days I'll punch that man,' he thought.

Upstairs, as she made her way along the hotel corridor, Judith met Irma coming in the other direction. The 'bronze Roman athlete' was pale beneath her tan, as if she had lost a lot of blood.

'Why did you just vanish from the Lido all of a sudden?' Judith asked.

Instead of answering, Irma took Judith's arm.

'Come downstairs with me.'

'Where to?'

'To the bar. For a drink.'

'Do I have to?'

'Yes.'

Irma sat her down in a big leather armchair and took a seat opposite. Both women ordered what Mr Lietzen always had: gin and vermouth.

'Dry Martini…'

It is a special kind of torture that young lovers always devise for themselves, to contrive a situation which puts them alone with the person who has caused their heartache. The victor.

'Did you enjoy yourselves after I'd gone?'

'We went swimming.'

'Immersing yourselves in happiness?'

Judith parried the unexpected blow. 'No. In the sea.'

Irma ordered two more dry Martinis.

'Didn't you miss me?'

'Yes.'

'You're lying, I don't believe you. How about a cognac?'

'Heavens, no!'

Judith is so prudent, Irma thought. She isn't the

gossiping type. She is always on her guard. She does her work so conscientiously. She's cleverer than me. And more devious. And more beautiful.

Irma was completely captivated by Judith's beauty, in the way that every truly feminine woman tends to overrate rather than dismiss the charms of her rival. She remembered the apparition of that afternoon, the marble limbs set off by the black bathing costume. In her mind's eye she kept imagining a tanned male arm embracing those snow white shoulders. A virginal imagination always tortures itself with superficies because those are the only things it knows. Its acquaintance with the full reality is purely through hearsay.

'It seems to me,' said Irma, 'that anyone who falls in love with a man for sensual, physical reasons must either be mad or over the hill. A young and healthy woman falls in love for other reasons—or often for no reason at all—and it's only when she's already *in* love that the physical side comes into play, of its own accord.' She thought about what she had said for a while and then added, 'And even then, not always.'

Judith said nothing. She really is on her guard, Irma thought. The bronze athlete in her could not stand this chilly marble temperament. She stood up.

'Come on,' she said, 'let's go for a walk. I'm feeling restless.'

'But—what about dinner?'

'We'll have some together, in an *osteria*. I've already arranged it all with Mother. She's having her evening meal in bed. There's something I want to tell you.'

They set off. It was already completely dark outside.

'We'll have dinner at Vida, on the square by San Giacomo dall'Orio. It's a good *osteria*.'

'Who recommended it to you?'

'A detective.'

She did not explain any further. She sensed that it sounded wild and mysterious. Judith walked beside her in silence, asking no questions. They set off in the direction of the railway station.

When strangers to Venice set off somewhere on foot, they tend to spend a lot of time wandering the narrow streets, crossing little bridges over unknown, nameless canals, until sooner or later they find themselves at the Grand Canal. There they get their bearings and set off into the warren of little streets again, until they come out at a different point on the Grand Canal. And so it goes on until finally they arrive at their destination. Thus it was that Irma and Judith made their way along the swollen waterways (it was that time in the evening when the high tide washes through the city and the lagoon waters seep inland, sluicing out the canals and leaving the bridges half submerged).

'Do you know where we're going?' Judith asked.

'As soon as we find the railway station we'll be there.'

They came out beside the Grand Canal. A *vaporetto* steamed past, its stumpy funnel belching not smoke but red-hot flames. At night time those funnels look like so many top hats sporting red feather garlands.

'Don't you agree with what I said about love?' said Irma. 'That love comes first, and only later develops into—well, you know...'

'Oh, absolutely.'

A single glance at Judith's expression in the dancing light of the smokestack flames would have been enough to show that deep down she did not remotely subscribe to that sorry virginal theory.

Crossing a handful of small bridges, they found themselves plunged in the medieval night-time of Venice. There is no other city in the world where the alleys are so eerily silent as in Venice after dark. After nightfall the blind brick walls, the colour of soot and of congealed blood, reach into the sky leaving just a slit of indigo high above them and slicks of jet black water below, silent and menacing. Here and there a wan yellow lamp pierces the gloom. A few paces further and the dark arches of a long bridge yawn in front of one. Suddenly the two girls felt gripped by fear. This kind of fear is never related to anything specific; it is more a fear of the unseen, of the invisible, warren-like world as a whole. Standing in those deserted, confined little streets gives one a feeling of nameless unease. Some of the streets are so narrow that you could shake hands from your window with your neighbour opposite. This whole area of the city is like a single ancient mansion, swathed in total darkness, its dim corridors drowned by floodwaters. The golden angels and the blue sky of St Mark's are a long way from here. It is as if they belonged to another world. The tiny, stepped bridges bring a little relief…

'You said you had something to tell me.'

'Yes,' said Irma nervously, 'but I'm too afraid out here. Let's hurry. I'll tell you when we get to the *osteria*. Oh, I wish we were there now, under a nice bright lamp!' And don't be too impatient, she appended silently. You won't like what I've got to say!

They hurried on. Another bridge. Then suddenly, unexpectedly, Irma stopped.

'Tell me,' she said, 'if you had a spare thousand *lire*, what would you spend it on?'

The biting tone of the question was met with a composed response.

'Baby linen. I saw some recently in a shop window in the Merceria. A complete layette.'

Irma stood motionless. The words struck at her heart. No sound at all could be heard by the bridge except for the intermittent slapping and sighing of the captive canal. Then, once again, the malevolent, secretive silence surged back. It was broken by Judith's quiet, painfully honest voice. It was almost as if she were speaking to herself, though her words were quite clear.

'I want a child.'

Irma's response was quieter still. 'I know what you want. I want it too.'

In the bygone Venice of the *Trecento*, a knife blade would have flashed at this point and a scream would have been heard. But now, seven hundred years later, there was not so much as a sigh. And then, from somewhere below them, piercing the long, deep silence, a mournful man's voice:

'*Oiè!*'

It was a gondolier, turning out of one canal into another, in the dead of night. His was a calm halloo, not a cry. A two-syllable communication from one human being to another. And after it, silence again.

'A child,' repeated Judith fervently, 'that's what I want. Ever since I went to the Frari church and saw that fat little naked three-year-old angel musician. It's in the sacristy, at the bottom of the altarpiece of the Madonna. There are two of them, a brown-haired one and a blonde, but it's the blonde one that I especially love, the one playing the flute. That adorable little curly head, the soft pink skin and the chubby little legs… They make you want to reach out and hug him. I want a child that looks just like that. Ever since I saw it, I've been looking at baby linen in shop windows. I'm completely obsessed with that tubby little angel…'

Irma was listening with full attention.

'Did Aurelian take you there, to the Frari?'

'Yes.'

'And did you go and look at the altarpiece together?'

'We did. It's exquisite. You should go and see it sometime.'

'No, I don't want to. It belongs to you.'

They continued on their way.

'Did you know that he had a lover?' Irma asked.

Judith's voice was wary. 'Who?'

'Oh, stop pretending!'

'Pretending?'

Irma stopped. 'All right, that's it!' she said indignantly. 'We've got to have this out now, tonight. I can't bear it a minute longer, I simply can't. Come on.'

Although Judith was taken aback by Irma's tone, she continued to follow where Irma led, emboldened by a sense of triumph, a sudden frisson that thrilled through her heart.

'It's not just idle gossip,' Irma went on, her voice loud in the deserted alleyway. 'The woman was here in Venice. Father heard about it from one of his people at the bank. He got her name, too. Lotte Welitsch.'

'Welitsch?'

'Yes. She's twenty-nine years old. From Vienna.'

She waited. Judith's face remained expressionless. Irma continued, trying to choose words that would cause pain.

'She was living in the same *pensione*. To all intents and purposes they were living together. She left the day before yesterday. They were having an affair.'

Judith's lips twitched into a frigid smile. 'I know.'

'You know? How?'

'He told me.'

This was an unexpected blow. And it made it certain, didn't it? If he had told her about this, then… All Irma's strength left her. She stopped on a small bridge and stood staring at the light of a distant boat, whose reflection in the water wriggled like a golden corkscrew. Suddenly she was seized by the need to know more. She would drag it all out of Judith. Her strategy would be to pretend that she knew it all already.

'A married woman.'

'Formerly married, yes. She was divorced.'

'Oh yes, well. Perhaps.' Irma's next words were spoken as a statement, though they were in fact a question. 'It was because of Aurelian that she stayed so long.'

'That's true. She came for a week and ended up staying a month.'

'But—but he sent her away so coldly.'

'Very.'

'She was a nice-looking woman. Pretty.'

It was not structured in the interrogative form, but once again it was a question. Again she waited. A gondola swished silently past under the bridge, looming like a large fish in the dark water.

'Her hair was black and she wore it parted in the middle,' Judith said. 'And she had beautiful lips.'

'Did you see her?'

'Of course not. He told me.'

'She loved him.'

'Yes.'

'But he didn't love her.'

'No.'

Irma waited to see if Judith would say any more. But Judith stayed silent until they reached the next bridge. Then, when they stopped again, she said quietly,

'She made a big mistake. She tried to make him marry her.'

As they stared down the length of the long canal they could make out two more bridges. Someone was standing on one of them, looking at them intently and in silence. He did not move.

'Let's get away from here,' whispered Judith.

They started walking again. The man was still standing on the bridge, in silence. They slunk into an alleyway. By now the route that Irma chose was completely haphazard. She wanted to make him marry her, she repeated to herself. But that's what *you* want, too. And it's what I wanted this afternoon. A cold shaft of pain seemed to travel from her heart to her knees, lodging itself there, making them tremble.

When they came to the next bridge, there was the man again, on another, parallel bridge, still silent.

'Are you scared?' Judith whispered.

Irma nodded. They hurried on. Their route took them over a wider canal. And suddenly, all was blinding light, accompanied by the fearful sound of machinery. Before them stood a dark red Gothic *palazzo* with its ground-floor traceried windows open onto the water. From inside came a dazzling white glare and a constant rumbling noise: it was a newspaper printer's, with rotary presses and workmen in shirtsleeves. Oh, the relief! The *palazzo*'s water gate was standing open. Inside it, under the vaulted entranceway, was a big barge filled with rolls of printing paper. On the further bridge they caught sight of the mysterious man again, and then he disappeared through a small door. An innocent newspaper editor—what a fright he had given them! They asked directions from one of the print workers, who was leaning out of a window to get some air. They set off.

'Interesting,' said Judith. 'I didn't know the woman's name, nor that she was Viennese. He didn't tell me that.'

'And all the rest, why did he tell you that?' asked Irma, a little too ready to sound accusing.

Judith was stung but her reply was calm and steady. 'Because I asked him point blank whether he had a lover.'

'What gave you the right?'

'Because I wanted a clear picture. Did he or didn't he?'

'But what gave you the *right*?' cried Irma again. 'What *right* did you have?'

'Please don't shout. Don't shout at me.'

Judith put some distance between them, running up the steps of a high bridge. Irma came after her. They stopped at the top. They stood face to face. Both of them were slightly out of breath. In a cold voice that shook a little, Irma asked,

'And—when did it happen…this conversation?'

'This afternoon.'

'On the Lido? After I'd gone?'

'Yes.'

They were once again surrounded by silence. The noise of the print works had long since faded away.

You *knew*, Irma thought, trembling. You knew just what swimsuit to put on in order to catechise him about his lover. You knew precisely how to steal him from me. She stood staring at Judith intently, as if she never planned to take her eyes off her. And then came the frank and painful question:

'Do you know why I'm asking you all this?'

'I think so, yes.'

Silence. Below them, from beyond the bridge, came the sound of lapping water. And a soft, benevolent voice:

'*Oiè!*'

The gondola swished past them, under the bridge, then disappeared around a distant corner. And at that moment, all of a sudden, something very odd happened. Irma darted forward, and with an untried, experimental movement gave Judith a shove that sent her reeling. The bridge had a parapet in the form of a low stone wall. Judith stumbled against it, scrabbling with her fingers, clutching at it convulsively. A fraction more momentum and she would have tumbled into the murky depths. Irma stood stock still, her hand on her heart, as pale as a ghost. Judith scrambled to her feet and slowly, methodically began dusting herself off. Then she turned a ghastly smile on Irma.

'Just what was all that in aid of?'

Irma had started crying, silently, her eyes closed. The

tears streamed down her upturned face. There could be no doubt about what had happened. She had tried to push Judith into the water. Sobbing, she uttered a barefaced lie.

'It was a joke.'

'No it wasn't,' said Judith, barely audibly.

Irma was still crying, surrendering herself to the monotonous, invincible rhythm of tears that she did not know how to stop. Her shoulders shook and her knees trembled. Feeling faint and weak, she laid her head against Judith's chest. Judith stroked her beautiful fair hair and stared out at the canal, where a solitary lamp was planting its twisted golden root in the black water. The silence seemed to go on forever.

And then, from the square very close to where they stood, the silence was suddenly rent by the thunderous tolling of the great bell of San Giacomo dall'Orio, and immediately after that the smaller bell, and then the two together, their twin booms slashing the veil of night, one succeeding the other, over and over, an ear-splitting din, a howl, a moan, on and on and on…

7

Mr Lietzen had to go to Trieste. He attempted to persuade his wife and daughter to go to the Tyrol or to Switzerland; it was beginning to get so hot in Venice. But every time he brought the subject up, the debate always ended with the same question:

'What do *you* think, Irma?'

And Irma always gave the same stubborn answer:

'I'd prefer to stay here.'

'All right, but for how much longer?'

'I don't know. For now I just want to stay here.'

And, as always, Mr and Mrs Lietzen let her have her way, though her father did try, experimentally, to advance a few objections.

'You're not sleeping well here, my dear. But in the mountains, you know, at one thousand eight hundred metres above sea level, you'd sleep like a top.'

Irma just smiled and said nothing. Was any mountain in the world high enough to help her sleep?

Mrs Lietzen took to watching her daughter closely while these holiday debates were going on. She had her suspicions as to why Irma wanted to stay in Venice 'for now', and thought she knew what was causing her sleeplessness. Reluctantly she let herself be persuaded. 'Very well,' she said, 'for now we will stay.' Her helplessly tender, elderly mother's heart could not bear to see the slightest flicker of suffering on her child's face. It is the source of so many problems, this maternal soft-heartedness, Mrs Lietzen knew it was. She was unable to resist the slightest whim her daughter might have. But what was she to do? It made her ill to see Irma suffer.

So Mr Lietzen went to Trieste, leaving his family behind. On the day of his departure, after lunch, a porter came to take his two small suitcases downstairs. He stood up to say goodbye.

'I'll see you to the station,' Irma said.

'My dear, how sweet of you!' cried her father in delight.

They went down to the quayside, to the landing stage for the motor boats. The porter followed with the luggage but it took them some time to get onto the water because a seething crowd had formed around the boat rank. People were practically pushing each other into the water.

'What's all this about?' Mr Lietzen wanted to know.

'*Amore*!' grinned a sailor.

Irma started at the sound of that word, as if someone had suddenly called out her name. At times like these, one is as responsive as a microphone.

They looked in the direction the sailor was pointing. Out on the lagoon, which sparkled in the sunlight, amid the hooting steamers, two gondolas were floating along, and leaning back against the cushions, under the burning sun, tail-coated and pomaded, a couple of stars from the Berlin film world were locked in passionate embraces with bleached blondes in ball gowns. The actors looked studiedly at the camera, which was trained on them from a motor boat in front of the gondolas, moving slowly and making sure to keep Venice in the background of each shot. From behind the camera, bespectacled film directors were testily shouting instructions in German, angrily stamping their feet and ordering the actors to be more lover-like, at which instruction the unfortunates launched themselves at each other once more, kissing fiercely and lengthily amid the bellowing and the noise from the steam boats and the roar of the motor engines and the commotion of the public on the quay. It was a revolting spectacle—but one should not judge too hastily; the skilful application of a blue colour filter and a background soundtrack of mandolins will transform a thing like this into the sweet sublimity of *Venice by Moonlight*, playing next winter in the Paramount Picture Palace. Pity poor Venice! Her beauty photographed to death, the repository of every newly-arrived lover's emotions—no matter that it is the long-dead Venice of the imagination with which they fall in love.

'*Amore!*' The sailor's loud, mocking voice echoed in Irma's ears even as she set off in the motor boat with her father. '*Amore!*' It was an ugly, rasping voice.

The boat swung round, turning away from the beautiful people sweatily feigning love for an hourly rate, and headed for the open lagoon, towards the Lido. This was not the way to the station. Irma touched her father's hand.

'Are you sure we're going the right way?'

'Yes, my dear. I'm not going by train.'

'Then how…?'

'I'm flying, my dear. But for pity's sake, not a word to your mother. Be a good girl and tell her I went by train.'

They were the only two passengers in the glass cage of the airport boat. Irma clutched her father's arm. Lietzen travelled so much that his family had ceased to feel any pangs of separation when he went. But now Irma was sorry to see him go. She hung on tighter to his arm. The boat raced towards the Lido, towards one of the three points on that long island through which the sea flows in, feeding its modest little cousin the lagoon. Irma was suddenly seized with the urge to tell her father everything, to pour her heart out there and then. Her father would be a good person to tell. It would never do to confide in her mother; her mother would just succumb to an attack of nerves, convinced that the world was falling to pieces. Her father was not like that. He was kind and clever and easy-going…

'Look!' Her father jolted her out of her reverie. He pointed to a place between the Lido and the small island of Sant'Andrea where a vast, wide channel had been cut, a sort of avenue in the ocean, straight as an arrow and glassy smooth with concrete sides, a runway for the seaplanes. It was the entrance to the *Idroscalo*, the Lido airfield, next to the military emplacements that guard the shoreline. A huge sign was printed with the word 'ADAGIO'. It was this and not the marine runway that Lietzen was pointing at.

'You see that lovely word on the sign there? What a wonderful language! What wonderful people! What sweet, bitter-sweet music comes to mind at the sight of that word. And yet all it means is "Slow down"!'

How Irma loved her darling, devil-may-care, music-loving Papa! He would understand her plight, she knew he would. Far better than any friend.

Behind the fortifications on the waterfront, strung out across a field of poppies, the brightly coloured seaplane hangars were coming into view. White walls, green swing doors and red roofs. Irma and her father disembarked while workmen in boiler suits took charge of the suitcases. Irma had already worked out what she was going to say:

'Daddy, don't go. I've got something to tell you.' Or perhaps not. Perhaps it would be better to say, 'Daddy, there's something you should know. If you want to hear it, don't leave now.'

Gleaming on the waterfront were two seaplanes, great silver animals with double sets of wings, held fast by stout ropes. Moored on their launch pads, their snub noses right up against the quay, they were lazily regarding the handful of passengers through their little glass-window eyes.

'That one's mine,' said Mr Lietzen, 'the *Falco*. That's what's taking me to Trieste. The other one goes to Fiume[18]. Have you got enough money?'

'Oh, plenty.'

'Have you spent the thousand *lire* yet?'

'Yes.'

'Splendid. What did you get with it?'

'It's a secret.'

She had a sudden idea. If I tell him what I spent it on, he'll abandon all thought of going away. We'll go and sit under that tree and I'll talk to him. We'll talk and talk until late in the evening…

The pilots came out of the hangar, clad in their yellow and green liveries, like jockeys before a race. Their ears were stuffed with cotton wool plugs and their front pockets bulged. Attaché cases swung from their hands. They climbed into their cockpits.

Now! she thought. I've got to say something now, while there's still time. She took a deep breath and began, very quietly. 'Daddy… I've got something…'

But just at that moment the two seaplane engines sprang into life. The pilots were testing them. Their roar completely drowned out the beginning of her whispered confession. Mr Lietzen stuck his fingers in his ears.

The first time in my life that I want to talk to him and he blocks his ears! Irma thought. She could have wept at the grotesque irony of it, at her sheer bad luck. The engines bellowed mercilessly, the backthrust of the propellers causing the water to fan outwards. It reminded her of a child blowing on a bowl of hot soup. If she had had the strength, she would have out-bellowed the engines, but her voice failed her.

'Daddy…? Daddy…!'

He could not hear her. The man in the boiler suit lowered the suitcases into the aeroplane and gave a sign to Mr Lietzen from the pilot ladder. He turned to kiss his daughter. Irma clung onto his neck, not wanting to let him go. The engines quietened down to a rumble.

'Bye-bye my dear,' said Mr Lietzen. 'Look after yourself.'

With that he climbed aboard, gave one last wave, and disappeared into the great silver maw of the machine. Two men manoeuvred the wooden steps away, another cast off the moorings and pushed the snub-nosed monster off from the quay. The *Falco* turned up the marine runway, in the direction of the open sea.

'Daddy! Daddy!'

Too late. Irma waved and shouted, as if crying for help. The engine roared, at full throttle once again. It stirred the water to a stiff foam as slowly the seaplane began to lumber towards the lagoon, the yellow and red of its upper wings glinting in the sunshine. After it came the other plane, bound for Fiume. Irma ran along the quayside, as if hoping to outpace them.

'Daddy! Daddy!' she shouted, 'Daddy, oh Daddy…!'

Her shouts were mingled with sobs but the silver monsters were too loud for her, and soon they left her far behind. The workmen took no notice. Desperate goodbyes, floods of tears—they were used to it.

From somewhere close by came the sound of cannon fire. The shoreline here was all military territory, heavily fortified, and there were always exercises in progress. And in the midst of all the booming ordnance and the roar of the engines, away went Mr Lietzen, the faithless father abandoning his grieving child. The seaplane had reached the end of its runway now. It turned. Impatiently, with a sudden furious blast of its engines, it began to rip through the water, seeming to tear the sea to shreds, and then it rose, shaking off the last stubborn, clinging filaments of liquid as it soared upwards into its true element. Swiftly, easily it was borne away into the radiance of the blue sky. Daddy had vanished out of sight.

Back in the motor boat once more, Irma huddled in the corner of the glass cabin. She had failed to make her confession. With a leaden weight still pressing on her heart, she let herself be carried back to Venice, rocking to and fro with the rhythm of the boat, back to the City of Suffering— Dante's name for Hell, the *Città dolente*. Far out to sea, along the horizon across which Mr Lietzen had flown, the brick-red sails were glowing again in the afternoon sun. From the direction of the now-distant fortress came the thundering of the cannons.

By five o'clock Irma was back under the arcades outside Caffè Florian, inspecting every customer. Aurelian was not among them. She went into St Mark's to pay a visit to the kneeling angel. Because Judith was not the only one with a favourite angel; Irma had one too. Hers was not a chubby little cherub but a slender, grave-faced, grown-up girl. She thought that perhaps she even preferred her to the golden-winged angels outside, the ones clambering up to Heaven along the roofline. To get to the kneeling angel you had to enter St Mark's by the furthest entrance door on the left. Then, once inside, after crossing the undulating mosaic floor in the gloom, you turned left in order to come out at the first chapel on the north side. The space is normally dark and narrow but at this time of day a single shaft of light came in through the lancet window in the thick end wall, falling on the altar and making the candlesticks gleam, lighting up the grave face of the kneeling angel, carved in relief on the altar frontal. Everything else was in deep shadow. The relief consists of angels kneeling on either side of a central cross, holding up censers towards it. Irma had got into the habit of coming here every day. She was particularly fond of one of the angels. A sweetly mournful, graceful messenger from Heaven with the face of a girl from a *Cinquecento* portrait. It was because of this that she liked it so much, because it was not an idealised face; it was clearly taken from life, modelled on the face of a real woman who had lived and breathed and suffered. How else could the sculptor have made that head so lifelike, with its slender neck and its high brow and its melancholy countenance? The model must have been the daughter of a great man. Only a noblewoman would have known how to kneel like that, so respectful and submissive, with such natural devotion, as if kneeling not in prayer but in reverence before a mighty Venetian doge, enthroned in regal splendour. Staring out with her five-hundred-year-old stone eyes, dimmed now with age, the expression on that angel's face seemed to transcend its own sacred symbolism and tangibly figure forth the flesh and blood face of that melancholy *nobildonna*, long since dead and crumbled to dust. Gradually, as the sun left the window, the face sank back into the shadows, to be enveloped once more by the golden gloom of the Byzantine basilica, consumed once again by the past...

Irma went back out into the radiant, bright, noisy square and the press of present-day humanity. Once again her eyes skimmed the faces seated at the little iron tables, until at last she found the one she was looking for. He was sitting in his usual place. She did not wait for him to invite her to join him. She simply went over and sat down, putting her hat on the table.

'Where have you sprung from?'

'I went to the airport to see Father off. He's flown to Trieste. Mother and I are staying here.'

Irma felt a kind of painful pleasure to be staying in Venice, Aurelian could read it in her eyes. He realised that he was terribly fond of her. He respected her, pitied her. He would never for the world let it show. What a fine thing it would be if this attractive, eager, bright young thing could sit here with him now as she had on that very first day.

She had lost weight. Her eyes, with that sweet, uneven gaze, had become more docile. They shone with a greater depth than formerly. The contours of her face seemed perceptibly more angular.

'I can't seem to sleep at the moment,' she said.

Aurelian was distressed to see her like this. He felt responsible. He leaned closer to her and asked,

'How is all this going to end, Irma?'

Bluntly and dispassionately, with the directness that comes of being robbed of all hope, Irma answered,

'Marry me?'

She placed her hand on his but she did not look at him. She did not even expect an answer. She knew that all she had done was give a name to her malady, nominate the cause of her insomnia.

Aurelian stared at the slim, well cared-for little hand that lay on top of his. 'I can't do that, Irma' he said.

'Because you love Judith.'

Aurelian did not reply. But his expression remained unaltered. It was an unspoken gesture of assent.

How cool and collected they are, Irma thought. So calm and yet—and yet we're talking of *love*. She took her hand away from his. They must have embarked on an affair, she told herself. They must have done, she was sure of it. She looked Aurelian full in the eyes, caring nothing for her own pride, just wanting to feel the prick of that electric current which lovers insist is a physical phenomenon but which modern science has yet to confirm. It crackled across her skin, she could feel it in her chest, around her lungs, between her shoulder blades, that stab of exquisite physical torture. If she closed her eyes for a moment it would be gone. If she looked at Aurelian again, it was like flicking a switch, triggering another painful surge. One could measure it in her pulse rate, she was sure. Was it right to be snatching this sensation from him? she wondered. She vindicated herself with the excuse that there was nothing erotic about it; it was pain not pleasure, like pressing on a wound. She looked away, switched the current off, and casually asked,

'What are you doing this evening?'

Very politely, Aurelian said, 'Nothing. I'm going home early.'

It was a rejection. Irma waited for a pretext, an 'I'm rather tired,' but none came. Nothing. She waited for a moment more, giving him time to add, 'But we could go out somewhere if you like.' But again nothing, nothing at all. She got to her feet.

'Are you going already?' was all he said.

'Yes.'

She picked up her hat, looked at him, smiled, shook out her mane of fair hair and went, without a word. Aurelian looked after her, solicitous, concerned. He followed her with his eyes until she was lost in the crowd. A lovely girl, he thought.

Back in the hotel, after dinner, Irma realised that Judith was nowhere to be seen. She went to her mother's room and almost tore the door down. Judith was not there either. Mrs Lietzen was undressing. Irma was on the point of asking where Judith was but she stopped herself and, in a slightly forced voice, said,

'Are you going to bed already?'

'Yes. I'm in a bad mood and I'm not feeling myself. This is the second time Mrs Lineman has let me down over Countess Morosini. Yet again she failed to get an invitation and instead took me off to some local inn where we ate a sort of fish soup, black as pitch, made from cuttlefish called *seppioline*. An ancient speciality, apparently. I've taken three magnesium tablets as a precaution. You know, I'm quite beginning to think that Mrs Lineman has never even met Countess Morosini.'

What do I care about Countess Morosini? thought Irma. Where's Judith?

Mrs Lietzen got into bed. 'That woman is beginning to get on my nerves with her local specialities that destroy my digestion and her countesses who won't receive us.'

Irma's nerves could stand it no longer. 'Where's Judith?' she burst out, trying too hard to sound unconcerned.

'I mean, really! Feeding a person black fish soup at five in the afternoon, I ask you!' grumbled Mrs Lietzen.

'Where's Judith?'

Finally she got her answer.

'Judith? She's getting changed. She wanted to go out on

her own tonight. For a walk. Or was it to go boating? I can't remember. Anyway, I've given her the evening off.'

'What, at ten o'clock?'

'Yes. It's far too hot during the day.'

Quietly, Irma shut the door and went back to her own room. So *that* was why Aurelian had nothing planned for the evening. *That* was why he was going home early.

She could not bear being alone in her room. Now that she was not sleeping, now that she was hardly eating anything, her nerves were constantly on edge. They would not let her rest, they were perpetually driving her on, keeping her active and awake. She snatched up her hat and went down to the lobby. She tried to avoid the hotel director but it was hopeless. She handed in her key and submitted to the director's obsequious greeting and his instantly attentive smirk, followed by the equally sudden relapse of his features into indifference.

'Is there something I can do for you, Miss?'

'Nothing, thank you. I just wanted to look at the telephone directory.'

'At your service, Miss. This way please.'

The director switched on the light in the telephone booth, indicated the directory hanging from its hook, flashed his instantly attentive smirk, then relaxed his features again and retreated.

Irma looked up the Corti guest house. It's funny, she thought, it's always my knees that give way first. Her legs were trembling again. Why was that? She took plenty of exercise, she swam, she played tennis. At home on the Danube she went rowing, too. She leafed through the telephone book. It must be the rowing, she told herself; it puts too much strain on the knee muscles. She squeezed her knees together to try to stop the shake. She found the number she was looking for and dialled it.

'*Pronto.*'

'Pensione Corti?'

'Yes.'

'I—I wanted to enquire whether you permit ladies to pay visits to gentlemen. Gentlemen guests of your establishment?' Her voice was cool and deliberate. She aimed to give the impression of being one such lady, desirous of paying a visit to a gentleman but first needing to know if it was possible.

'Yes.'

'I beg your pardon, did you say yes?'

'Yes. By all means. Provided that the gentleman has no objection...'

'Thank you.'

She came out of the telephone booth and went into the reading room, sitting down on the nearest sofa. They were having an affair. Judith had gone to him. In her mind she went over Judith's words of the night before. 'She made a big mistake. She tried to make him marry her.' Judith was cleverer than the Viennese woman. Judith considered it a mistake to try to get a man to propose. Judith knew that Aurelian could not be trapped that way. Judith became his

155

lover. Mockingly, Irma's lips formed the words that had been exchanged between her and Aurelian. 'What are you doing tonight?' 'I'm going home early.'

She got up and went back to the lobby. Acting as if she had no particular plan, she walked up and down a bit, but all the time looking hard at the little compartments behind the front desk. Some had keys in them, some not, according to whether the occupant of each room was in or out. Judith's number was 120. The key was hanging on its hook. Judith had left the hotel.

'Yes, Miss?' said the concierge.

'My key, please. Number 112.'

And when the concierge turned to reach for it, she added coolly, 'And the nurse's key as well, please. Number 120.'

She was handed both keys. She went up in the lift and headed straight to Judith's room. She had only seen it once before, on the day they arrived, when they were deciding who would sleep where. Judith's room looked onto the inner courtyard. Irma switched on the light. It looked like a neat housemaid's room. She began searching through the contents, freezing in fright, like a thief, each time she heard footsteps in the corridor. She had no clear idea of what she was looking for. She just knew that she wanted to—to intrude on this girl's privacy. And to see if she could find something that might relate to—*that*. Her imagination was so overwrought, she was obsessed with her suspicion. Every insignificant little scrap of paper must offer a clue, she felt. She was glad that the tiny room was so full of things to look through. One of them would surely turn out to be significant. She rummaged through drawers, looking for letters, scribbled notes. She found nothing. In the desk drawer there was a little notebook but it contained nothing but telephone numbers. She read through them carefully. No secrets there. They were the numbers of companies in Vienna and Budapest, one or two familiar family names. She opened the wardrobe. Underwear, in neat piles. Blouses. No—no! She shut the door firmly. She was beginning to warm to her task. She threw open the large, dark green travelling trunk. It was not locked, there would be nothing interesting in there, she thought. She was right. It was full of shoes, carefully stored on their lasts and wrapped in shoe bags. Shoes that would not be needed in Venice. Shawls, scarves, clutch bags, books, a thousand dull pieces of nothing. She scrabbled through it all irritably, almost annoyed with Judith for having nothing worth finding. Then she carefully put everything back the way she had found it. Where are they now, what are they doing now? The question pursued her, round and round. She went on with her search. On the bedside table she found a photograph of a little child. It was Bellini's fat little angel musician, one of its pudgy legs raised on a step, puffing out its cheeks as it blew into its flute. This was what Aurelian had taken Judith to see in the Frari. 'I want a child like that,' Judith had said. In the bedside drawer she found her mother's medicines, mainly sleeping pills, which Mother was not allowed to keep in her own room because she would take too many at once. A box of Italian wax matches. An envelope full of prescriptions. And something else: the string of wine-red beads that Judith had bought that evening, purely because Irma had not liked them. Against her snow white neck and her jet black hair they had suited Judith horribly well, Irma was prepared to admit it now... She rummaged further. It was only a shallow drawer, the kind you always find in hotels, usually with headed notepaper in them. There was notepaper in this one too and a post office slip, the receipt for a registered letter. A letter to an address in Vienna, to a woman with a German name at the Rudolfineum. A message from one nurse to another. There was more besides. A pile of picture postcards, stacked neatly on top of each other, addressed to Judith and arranged in date order. Salzburg, Innsbruck, Brennero, Cortina d'Ampezzo... A motoring holiday. Each of the postcards bore the same message: 'Warm wishes from R.'

R.

Judith has experience when it comes to men, Irma said to herself, staring at the boldly traced capital letter. R. She doubted if R was the first or even the only one. Judith is experienced, Irma thought, and that is the great advantage she has over me. Irma was certain that Judith was in the Pensione Corti now, with Aurelian. She had never left the hotel on her own before. Today was the first time. She had a perfect right to do so, of course. She was an independent woman. A woman who worked for a living.

Carefully, Irma put the postcards back where they had come from. She left the room, shutting the door behind her, then went back down to the lobby and handed in both keys. Feeling a little ashamed of her furtive search through Judith's belongings and aggrieved by how little it had yielded (a circumstance she attributed to Judith's sly cunning), she almost tore open the door of the telephone booth. She felt tortured by the need to do something, to act somehow. Curiosity was gnawing at her, sending her into a frenzy. Where were they? What were they doing? Once again she asked the operator to put her through to the guest house.

'*Pronto.*'

'Pensione Corti?'

'Yes.'

'I'd like to speak to *Dottore* Aurelio Szabó.'

There was a long silence. Nobody came to the telephone. Then, at last, 'There's no answer from his room.'

Irma slammed down the receiver and rushed out into the night. She was beside herself. She didn't even think to put her hat on, she kept it clutched in her hand. She ran forward a few paces, then stopped, then went slowly on again, then broke into a run once more. Then, at long last, she saw the sign in front of her. Black letters above a low glass door: Pensione Corti. She went in.

The guest house was respectable but down-at-heel—extremely so. Her first reaction was one of pained surprise. Such a shabby place for a man as well turned-out as

Aurelian always was. Was this really where he lived? There were a couple of basket chairs, two little tables covered in cloths with a printed flower design, one of them stained with coffee, the other with a nickel matchstick holder with no matches in it. The dourness was relieved only by the lamp hanging from the low ceiling: a riot of glass flowers. Venice… At the back of the entrance hall was a little glass door marked 'Office'. Beside it a steep, narrow staircase led upwards, up to the room where…

'Poor people such as ourselves…'

She had had to send to the kitchen for the concierge. She had found a flunkey in a green apron and shirtsleeves hanging about the hall but he had not been able to answer any of her questions.

'The concierge is in the kitchen. I'll get him…'

This had been followed by a whiff of cooking smells, of frying oil, *frittura*. She thought of her own five-hundred-year-old palace hotel with its proud, tomato-red, marble encrusted façade and its lobby, resplendent in gold and cast iron and mahogany and glass mosaic, where a jazz band played discreetly amid the potted palms. Suddenly the idea of it filled her with revulsion. Her heart longed to be here, with the coffee-stained tablecloth, where they could sit quietly in the afternoons, just the two of them, poor and undisturbed, each in a basket chair. Her soul was seized with a desire felt by so many wealthy young women: the yearning to be poor. As poor as the person one loves. Not to have to blush any longer for all the pampered luxury of her existence, luxury which must seem like a kick in the teeth to someone who lived in a place like this. And Judith, Judith… Judith would feel completely at home here, completely at her ease in this freer, truer, fresher, younger world…

The concierge appeared, wiping his mouth.

'I'm looking for *Dottore* Aurelio Szabó,' said Irma, beginning to tremble as she spoke. 'Is he here?'

The concierge glanced at the cubby holes behind the entrance desk. 'No. His key is here.'

'Which—which one is his?'

'That one. Number 19.'

There was a Hungarian newspaper in the cubby hole too, and a couple of letters.

'He's not in, I tell you,' said the concierge irritably. 'He went out this morning and hasn't returned since then.'

'Are you sure?'

The concierge gestured impatiently at Number 19. 'There's his midday mail, still not picked up.'

'Thank you.'

Sometimes life is capable of understated little gestures of consolation, like the one conveyed by those words. Irma looked up at the old-fashioned wall clock above the concierge's head. It was eleven o'clock. She left the building, lingering a little outside the door to steady her nerves. She heaved a ragged sigh and looked back through the glass door at that quiet, peaceful, shabby place as if it were a happier world than her own but somehow completely out of her reach. That feeling had begun to germinate when the three of them had stood looking at that bracelet in the jeweller's window. She had fallen in love with the idea of being poor. She felt now, for the second time since she had come to Venice, that she would simply like to throw all her belongings away, to embrace poverty—quite independently of Aurelian. Irma was not unique in this. The immature hearts of the pampered young rich are often seized by a yearning to be poor. The wealthy laugh at them for this, as do those who know what poverty really means. But one has to reach a certain age before one fully learns to appreciate worldly goods. For spoiled young rich people, still semi-children, this sudden mad lust to have nothing is not an imposture or a pose. Their yearning might be less intense but it is no less genuine than the yearning once felt, in Italy, by the profligate, prodigal, damask- and velvet-clad son of a rich textile merchant, who at the age of twenty, befuddled by wine and women, was suddenly possessed by a fervour so great that it propelled him to Heaven. In the town of Assisi, this young man cast off his silks and velvets for the meanest, filthiest rags. His name was Francesco di Bernardone. St Francis.

Irma, though, like so many before her, got no further than the sighing and repining. She tried to fly but she only had a chicken's wings. As one who re-offends and returns to jail, so she too went back to her palace hotel.

8

Mrs Lietzen and her daughter were getting ready for the German poet's *soirée*. It was to be held in what was widely considered the finest *palazzo* in Venice. The German poet rented part of it (twenty-three rooms) and was in the habit of throwing grand summer parties there, with an international guest list. Gaunt and ginger-haired, with milky blue eyes behind thick spectacles, the German poet was a global bird of passage. When in Venice, he aimed to support a phenomenon that was otherwise in its death throes: the *beau monde* social life of the grand *palazzi*. Normally what one hears, when enquiring after this or that now-impoverished patrician Venetian family, is that 'they are not at home' or 'they live in very reduced circumstances', or that for the summer they have rented their *palazzo* to a family of North Americans. The German poet, however, threw a number of summer *soirées*. And on each occasion his windows on the Grand Canal shone with the brilliance of yesteryear and all night long a veritable horde of boatmen and gondoliers lounged by the *palazzo*'s water gate, between the striped mooring poles with their gilded coats of arms.

The poet passed diffidently from guest to guest—he hardly knew most of them; he gave these parties out of love for Venice, out of the sheer goodness and simplicity of his heart. He caused the Venice that he knew and adored to rise from the ashes, in all its past glory, and he offered society beauties, American film stars, writers, bankers and sporting champions the chance to relive its glamour.

Mrs Lietzen was feeling much better and had accepted the invitation with alacrity. Her keenness was also partly to do with the fact that she was disappointed in Mrs Lineman. That lady had only once managed to obtain access to a real *palazzo*. Admittedly it had been to take tea with the Princesse de Polignac but still, the vaunted, celebrated Countess Morosini remained elusive. Mrs Lineman had yet to deliver on that promise and it was wounding to Mrs Lietzen's *amour propre*. Not that she was not still fond of the American lady. Since Venice first existed, no two matrons can have squabbled more fiercely over what price to accept for a gondola ride. And things like that bring old hearts together. Like the episode in the draper's establishment where they had haggled so long over twenty metres of golden brocade that they had literally been thrown out of the shop. The proprietor had finally realised that they had no intention of buying; they were just enjoying running their fingers over all the costly fabrics. The experience had given them a bond. Sighing in unison and linking arms, they had gone on their way. The only real sticking point in the friendship was Mrs Lineman's culinary mania. On the grounds that she was 'very partial to fish', Mrs Lietzen had been prepared to forgive the *passarini*, fried in oil in the time-honoured Venetian style, despite the fact that they were stuffed with a mess of onions and raisins. But she had drawn the line at the other thing, the *seppioline* fish soup. That had been unpardonable. It made no difference how hard Mrs Lineman protested that the ghastly black sauce was completely traditional, made from the unfortunate cuttlefish's own ink.

Despite this *contretemps*, they had nevertheless agreed that they would see each other at the German poet's and they had made a pact to dress to the nines.

At nine o'clock Aurelian came up to the Lietzens' suite. He was wearing black tie. He had also received an invitation to the *soirée* and had come to fetch the ladies. He waited in the living-room while they were putting the finishing touches to their finery. Irma was dressing in the room to the left; Mrs Lietzen, assisted by Judith, in the room to the right. When Judith came in to speak to Aurelian, he caught a glimpse of her mistress, seated in front of her silver-framed dressing mirror, arrayed like a duchess in a shimmering golden gown. She was painstakingly primping her pride and joy, her halo of bleached white hair.

'Is Irma still getting ready?' asked Aurelian, when Judith had closed Mrs Lietzen's bedroom door behind her.

'Yes,' said Judith with an amused smile. 'It's taking her quite a while. She refuses to let me help her.'

'Did you use to help her dress?'

'Always.'

'And tonight?'

'She shooed me away. Almost as if she were denying me a favour. She scarcely speaks to me now, just a word here and there. I'm beginning to find the situation unbearable. It would have been better if they had gone away, as originally planned. It was never part of the agreement that I would go with them. I would have stayed behind.'

From her composed, white face the Ottoman eyes looked tenderly and lovingly up at his. They stood facing each other. Aurelian took a step forwards. Judith lifted her hand and began adjusting his bow tie. They were standing very close. Judith fidgeted nervously with the tie, and then, for no apparent reason, undid it altogether.

'You would have stayed behind?' Aurelian said.

Judith nodded. She began to refasten the tie in a neat bow. Aurelian felt a sudden surge of male triumph, invigorating and sweet. Tauntingly, he savoured it.

'To see more of Venice?' he asked.

Judith shook her head.

'What, then?'

Judith looked at him, shrugging her shoulders, still fiddling with his tie. Aurelian moved his face even closer to hers.

'Nino?' he whispered.

Judith's head went up. She dropped her hand and took a step backwards. Aurelian closed the distance between them again.

'Don't be angry…'

Judith lifted a warning finger, looking towards Irma's door. Aurelian stepped away from her, raised his hand to his tie with a little cough. It might have been a coded message of secret love.

The door opened and Irma walked in. She came to a standstill under the chandelier, undoing the buttons on a pair of brand new, long white gloves. She looked beautiful, dressed up ready for the ball in a crisp, sweet-smelling gown, completely smooth and without a single crease. The hundred little fidgeting adjustments of the last half hour, experimenting in front of the mirror, craning backwards, bending forwards, looking now this way now that, the final close-up scrutiny when one moves so close to the mirror that the tip of one's nose touches the tip of one's nose—all this had produced a smiling sense of confidence. 'I'll do,' the woman tells herself. A moment of calm before the battle has to be joined.

Irma was wearing a floor-length plain white raw silk dress fastened by a velvet collar in a shade of smoky raspberry, which left her shoulders bare. Her sun-bronzed face was paler than before and more expressive. She fixed her attention intently on her gloves, slowly and painstakingly unfastening the buttons as if it were the most important task in the world. It felt painfully awkward to be standing there in her exquisite dress, opposite the freshly shaven man in his dinner-jacket and the poor little orphan girl in black who, like Cinderella, was staying at home while the glittering gentlefolk went to the ball. And yet she could not help a momentary, fleeting sense of spiteful triumph. Without looking at Judith she could feel her assessing eyes upon her. I know how to carry off an evening gown, she thought, undoing the final button on her gloves. For a brief moment she allowed herself to enjoy the silent admiration of the bank clerk and the nurse but then a sudden idea occurred to her: 'The princess has gilded her breasts.' Her lips gave an imperceptible little twitch of self-mockery.

'How lovely you look,' said Judith truthfully.

Still not looking up from her gloves, Irma replied coldly, 'Don't lay it on so thick.'

That had been unnecessarily rude. But in the light of the sparkling, opulent Venetian chandelier, looking at herself in the mirror opposite and drawing herself up taller and more erect, conscious of her elegance and her beauty, she felt somehow transported into the greasepaint world of a ham-acted French drawing-room melodrama. Her manner and her voice accordingly took on a note of false, frigid hauteur. Childishly she imagined a world of stock characters: the 'heartless beauty', the 'haughty ice queen', the 'siren'. She had entered a realm of 'level gazes' and 'heated passion', succumbing to a false, overwrought, fictional notion of noble heartbreak into which she had been thrown by the blazing chandelier, by her figure-hugging ball gown and its reflection in the mirror.

Judith made no response to the insult. Aurelian looked at the carpet in confusion. Irma behaved as if nothing had happened, speaking with the assumed insouciance of a beautiful actress, still looking at herself in the mirror.

'I managed to get ready all on my own.'

This caught Aurelian's attention. 'Why all on your own?'

'Oh, I can't bear the feeling of being fiddled with. You know—when someone's trying to get you into all this…' She gestured at her dress, her hand sweeping her figure from shoulder to toe. 'It just has a negative effect.'

'What do you mean by a negative effect?' asked Judith, her voice completely dispassionate.

Irma's reply was stiff and cold (it was the dress that did it). 'I don't know, it's just a feeling. If someone touches me— if people touch me—touch my skin, it—it's like when you tinker with a badly wired lamp and it gives you an electric shock.'

Judith left the room.

Aurelian began slowly pacing up and down. He glanced briefly out of the window before turning to Irma.

'Why are you so beastly to her?'

The 'haughty ice queen' just stared at him. 'Do you really need to ask?'

Guiltily, Aurelian dropped his gaze. 'You should try to control yourself,' he said.

'Controlling myself isn't good for me. Mother understands that. No one else does. It's better if I give things free rein. If

I try to bottle them up, I explode.'

'But it makes things so unpleasant for everybody else. And there's no need for it. Everyone is terribly fond of you.'

Easing herself into her long gloves, she said, 'A waiter in Cannes once said to Father, when he saw him looking longingly at a cucumber salad that he didn't dare risk eating, "Everyone is very partial to cucumber, but cucumber is partial to no one."' Gently she massaged her fingers into place inside the snow-white gloves. She did not speak. When all ten fingers were done and the top button of each glove was fastened on her upper arm, she no longer had anything to do. She walked across to where Aurelian was standing. Her cheeks were burning. She moved closer, a little awkwardly but so suddenly that Aurelian thought she was going to kiss him.

'This can't go on,' she said in a low whisper.

It was the first time they had stood together like this, dressed as if for an elegant costume drama, in ball gown and black tie. Still in the whisper, but almost as if she were threatening him, Irma went on,

'Tonight, when we get to the party, I'm going to make you tell me everything. We'll have a *tête à tête*, just the two of us. We've got to clear things up.' And then, on a deep sigh, she repeated, 'This can't go on.'

Aurelian forced himself to meet her eye without looking away. He made no reply.

Relentlessly, Irma went on, bluntly firing a question at

him. 'Do you love her?'

Aurelian's response was evasive. 'Why are we torturing each other?'

But Irma just repeated her question, louder this time. 'Do you love her?'

With a straight face he gave her a straight answer. 'Why ask the question when you know the answer perfectly well?'

'Do you plan to marry her?'

'Absolutely.'

Irma looked over his shoulder at the mirror, as if asking it for help. There stood the white-gowned, crimson-collared, 'haughty ice queen', someone who would never allow herself to grovel. Once again the beautiful dress came to her rescue. Coolly, almost indifferently, she managed to say,

'I'm sorry to hear it. Very sorry indeed. Because without you, I'm not sure there's any point to my existence.'

9

They left the party at eleven o'clock because the heat was so unbearable that Mrs Lietzen almost fainted. The guests—or at any rate as many of them as could find a space—were sitting by the marble windows on the Grand Canal, grateful for some fresh air. A colossal crowd was packed into the twenty-three rooms. The guests were well stoked with wine and champagne and in turn the heady atmosphere was stoked by the guests. A few couples were still resolutely taking turns around the dance floor. Other guests were equally resolutely gulping down glassfuls of fiery Italian wine. Italian wines soak up such vast amounts of sunshine on the vine that anyone who drinks them turns bright pink, as if the sunshine were shining back out again. Only one or two true connoisseurs noticed that the German poet had put together a purely Venetian *carte des vins*. This was not the typical bland Italian wine selection that one encounters in hotels. These were genuine Venetian vintages, made from ancient, historic grape varieties. The blonde Prosecco, grown on the slopes of neighbouring Conegliano; and the purple Friularo, celebrated in ballads from two centuries ago. The scrawny director of one of Berlin's state-financed art galleries found himself reduced to tears as he drank, appreciatively deeply; but most of the guests just took what they were given and milled obliviously around the heaving salons, for the thousandth time remarking what a mistake it had been to invite quite so many people.

It was an international gathering, mottled with splashes of cosmopolitan colour. There was a black-and-white group: men in dinner jackets swarming around the broad tuxedo of a celebrated movie mogul. There was a gash of scarlet silk draped across the otherwise naked body of a bony blonde. Then there was a silver gown that reached to the floor, entirely covering its wearer's toes before suddenly evaporating above the waist, relinquishing the upper body to a sort of slender silver harness which sliced furrows across a pale, fleshy midriff, leaving no scope at all to the imagination. The elderly wife of an Indian maharajah had submitted her noble Brahmin forehead to the surgical insertion of a single central ruby. Swathed in green, with a golden shawl about her head, her stout proportions resembled nothing so much as a magnum of champagne. A beautiful but vapid Hollywood star, the most ravishing of all the ladies present, was so perfect in her beauty that it sounded the death knell of all desire. The girlishly slim wife of a British former Prime Minister had had a facelift so successful that from her profile one would have put her age at sixteen. Face-on she looked every day of fifty-eight. Whiffs of the latest French fragrances mingled in the heat like a migraine-inducing incense.

The host flicked like a lounge lizard from room to room, ginger-haired, slim and debonair, his eyes darting here and there from behind his spectacles. At one of the windows he stopped to speak to a madcap little sixteen-year-old American girl who sat precariously balanced on the windowsill, hanging on his every word but nevertheless—with calculated disregard—paying no attention at all to her diaphanous gown, which had fallen open above her knees. The German poet was addicted to risk. Like his elder brother the flying ace, he was impervious to danger, to distance, to height. His brother had piloted the first primitive aircraft, dicing with death amid the clouds even after nine out of ten of those aircraft had crashed. The poet had chosen his own brand of derring-do. He was a writer. He wrote plays. And nine out of ten of them had flopped. It was his addiction to risk that had made him rent this *palazzo*. Purely on a whim, twenty-three rooms in a building famed in the annals of art history. And then he had embarked on another perilous journey: he had travelled the length and breadth of northern Italy, visiting every double-dealing antiques merchant he could find, and had fitted up those twenty-three rooms in period style. Which led him on to the most dangerous journey of all: drumming up the money to pay for it all. It was for that reason that the sixteen-year-old American minx interested him so much. Apart from that, he paid little attention to his guests. He knew perfectly well that for them, the real draw was the Renaissance *palazzo*. It was that, and

174

not he, who was the true host this evening.

Most of the guests belonged to that itinerant class that has been on the move since the war, migrant human swallows glumly traipsing the globe, grouping and regrouping so often that they all know each other, if not personally, then at least by name or by sight. Germans, Danes, English, Viennese, Belgians, Poles, White Russians, Americans who have decamped to Europe, none of them staying still, all on the move for their own different reasons, forever running into each other, to the extent that they bore each other to tears. Elderly ladies with lusty young squires; the divorcée baroness travelling with her mother; the dejected wallflower, paraded for sale by her ever-hopeful parents; the ageing but still beautiful 'singer' with a daughter in tow, learning the secrets of her mother's trade; the rich but talentless composer with his much younger wife; the retired spiv; the morphine-addicted Polish countess; the now distinctly doddery former England cricket champion—a bridge-partying, yachting, motoring, golf-playing, hotel-dwelling sorry little band, all living out of portmanteaux, flocking to Hanselmann's in Saint Moritz on winter mornings, or lounging in the card room of the Winter Palace in Luxor; running into each other in Van Dongen's studio in Paris or in Reinhardt's Marble Hall in Salzburg; irritated to see each other yet again in Rome, in the selfsame line for an audience with the Pope; recognising each other's unclad forms on the Lido's Excelsior beach; clustered round the Gennaro-Bourbon table at the

Ambassadeurs in Cannes or delicately grimacing as they sip tepid curative water on the flower-filled terrace of the Schlossbrunn in Karlsbad. More recently they have tried to escape each other by heading for Jerusalem, with the result that they all find themselves once more reunited round the evening card tables in the King David Hotel, until at last the *Vulcania* sets sail for Genoa.

Apart from Fred and Bunny, Mrs Lineman and the handsome Nino, the Lietzens knew almost no one. It being late, the two baby-faced honeymooners were as lively as crickets. Cross-eyed from drinking enormous quantities of champagne, they danced with each other incessantly, not romantically but diligently and precisely, rehearsing the steps they had been taught at school, focusing all their attention on where they were putting their feet. Looking over the top of her *pince-nez*, Mrs Lineman rattled off her explanation as to why Count Dolfin Boldù could not receive them. It was because he had gone off to Africa on a lion hunt. Franchetti was part of the same expedition. Though it was important to be aware of the difference in rank. Franchetti was merely a baron, whereas Dolfin Boldù was something even more exalted than a count because Venetian patricians of truly ancient lineage put the letters 'N.H.' in front of their names, standing for '*Nobilis Homo*'. But baron or no baron, *nobiluomo* or not, the fact was that both men were passionate lion hunters—known for it the world over. But as soon as they got home again Mrs Lineman could guarantee…

Nino brought Irma a glass of champagne and Irma introduced him to Aurelian. Aping the manner of the Lietzens' hotel director, Aurelian smirked falsely at the Italian officer and did not address a single word to him all evening. Irma danced with Aurelian once, but she did not enjoy the experience. The advantage that modern dance brings, she thought, allowing one to hold the person one loves in one's arms, is completely cancelled out by the fact that one cannot look him in the eye. She had assumed that dancing with Aurelian would be her chance to talk to him. But Fred and Bunny, who were still looking devotedly at their feet, kept dancing into everyone. The slow, alternate, gliding rhythm of all the other dancers, which usually allows each couple to exchange short bursts of meaningful conversation, was entirely destroyed by them. The only time Irma and Aurelian exchanged a word was when they found themselves trapped in a knot of dancers and had to wait for it to dissolve. Held at a forced standstill in Aurelian's arms, Irma looked up at him and, emboldened by the champagne, said,

'How did you express it, in the hotel just now, when you said you planned to marry Judith? Absolutely, was that the word?'

'Absolutely, Irma.'

'And me? What about me?'

Her eyes burned into his, hungry for an answer.

'You… Let me go, Irma. Let us be.'

They were dancing again.

'Never!' said Irma. 'Never!'

Aurelian felt the hand he was holding turn to ice. The next moment she had left him and gone back to her mother, who was sitting with Mrs Lineman. Nino, with well-bred patience, was keeping the two old ladies entertained. He was a local boy, born and bred in Venice, and was now explaining to them, with a certain heartfelt rancour, how hurtful it was the way Americans seemed to assume that the Venetians were nothing but a bunch of idle tour guides, living off the legacy of Titian and Sansovino, when in fact it was not the sight of St Mark's Square that quickened the heartbeat of every true-born modern Venetian (with due respect to antiquity, of course) but the magnificent, brand new port of Marghera, which they themselves had built. And those same true-born modern Venetians, quite rightly, did not see why hundreds of poor Venetian children should have to die of tuberculosis and rickets just so that foreign sightseers should not be deprived of the picturesque and romantic sight of damp, decaying five-hundred-year-old houses.

Mrs Lietzen was only half listening. What does this fellow want me to do? she asked herself irritably. I'm not the League of Nations. The heat was affecting her temper and it distressed her to see her daughter so restless and fretful, her apparent exuberance so forced and false. Aurelian hung around them, wordlessly mopping his forehead. Nino was making himself much more agreeable, and it was precisely for that that Mrs Lietzen disliked him. For that and other things.

Next to Mrs Lietzen sat Mrs Lineman, burbling like the engine of an idling motor car. But she was sawing off the very branch on which she sat. She knew how hysterically sensitive Mrs Lietzen was to the slightest small shock and yet once again she had brought up the subject of that frightful black cuttlefish soup and—to add insult to injury—had started chattering about lunching tomorrow in some sort of hostelry where they serve yet another variety of ancient Venetian pottage whose name, when she uttered it, made even the Italians look at her in alarm: *zuppa di peoci*. Not to mince words, it translates as 'louse soup', a name made even more unappetising by the fact that these *peoci*, these marine bloodsuckers, are supposedly tasty and nutritious. Ugh! cried Mrs Lietzen to herself. Still no Countess Morosini and yet instead she offers me this revolting soup? She began to wonder if the time had not come to break off relations with the American lady. This latest soup idea was really beyond the pale.

Mrs Lineman's prattle made Nino laugh. Irma had sat down in front of him and now, boldly tipping her chair right back, she stared flirtatiously up at his face. Mrs Lietzen's eyes were continually on her daughter. Nino had secreted a bottle of champagne in the window alcove and he was using it to keep the ladies' glasses topped up. He himself hardly drank. But after a while he grew irritable, beginning to hate this unknown Hungarian bank clerk who just stood there without saying a word to him. He remembered how Aurelian had glared at him on the boat, when he had spoken to Judith. It seemed that nothing was going right this evening. A blob of pink ice cream had melted into a large stain all over Irma's gown. Irma laughed but her mother was vexed. Then a fat Viennese lawyer came over, bowed obsequiously low and kissed Mrs Lietzen's hand, before realising that he had mistaken her for someone else. Irma saw Aurelian look surreptitiously at his watch.

And then came a burst of sudden panic. Mrs Lietzen screamed.

'My brooch!'

She had lost her brooch. The one with the large hazelnut-sized black pearl in the middle and two equally large diamonds on either side, with a circlet of twenty one-carat blue-white diamonds round the edge.

But in the next instant it turned up, lying right in front of them on the *terrazzo* floor. On close inspection it was found that the clasp was not fastening properly. Mrs Lietzen put it in her bag and Mrs Lineman began talking about how to get it repaired free of charge.

'Any large jeweller will do a job like that for nothing,' she purred, 'because they'll be hoping to get…'

Mrs Lietzen whispered to her daughter in Hungarian that she would do her American friend an injury one of these days if she couldn't stop talking for two minutes together.

Irma felt the champagne going to her head. She resolved that from tomorrow she would take up drinking regularly. The pangs of unrequited love had become unbearable and alcohol had such a pleasant way of dulling them. She felt light-headed and a little giddy—and Nino was so good-looking.

I'll adopt a promiscuous way of life, she told herself, savagely merry. Now it's *my* turn to teach *men* how to suffer. And she gave the young Italian leaning over her such a look that even he was startled. It had been a hair's breadth more wanton than was seemly.

'Would you like to dance?' Nino asked at once.

In lieu of a reply, Irma stood up and hurried off to join the dancers. Then, turning round, she smilingly slithered into Nino's arms. Fred and Bunny crashed into them and, as they stood still a moment to let the amorous infants go past, Nino pressed his burning cheek close against Irma's own. The 'haughty ice queen' did not pull away. She tolerated his proximity, lowering her eyes a little and repeating to herself: 'Burning passion'. She felt so light-headed she could have taken off with Nino to the clouds. He was a superb dancer.

'What's your name?' she whispered in his ear, fully aware of how hot her breath was.

The Italian laughingly told her. His name was not Nino. It was Domenico.

'Do you know what I call you?' Irma whispered.

'Yes. Nino.'

'How do you know?'

'Your friend told me.'

'Oh. And how do you like my—my friend?'

'Not as much as I like you.'

'I don't believe you.'

'It's the truth, I swear!'

Gaily, frivolously, coquettishly she laughed, putting a bit of distance between their faces so as to look into his eyes. I'm a loose woman, she told herself, in between their bouts of French and Italian dialogue. Loose and libidinous… She enjoyed the way the words sounded. She looked back to where she had left her mother. Aurelian was still standing there, watching her intently. They went on dancing.

'He can't take his eyes off you,' said Nino.

'Can't he?'

'I think he's jealous.'

'Oh, I doubt it…'

The dancing had expanded into the next room, though so far only one couple had taken advantage of the fact. Nino began to steer Irma in that direction.

'Where are you taking me?'

'Away from the crowd.'

He led her into the adjoining room. It fitted well with the theme of 'burning passion', Irma thought, to be borne away, to be carried off, to be abducted… A long enfilade of brightly lit rooms opened off the second ballroom. Nino began to guide her, still dancing, towards the first of them. Irma laughed. A fat tear had sprung to her eye.

'Do you know what I want, Domenico?'

'Call me Nino.'

'Do you know what I want, Nino? I want to die.'

Desperately, beseechingly, intoxicated with all the pent-up humiliation of her adolescent passion, the searing pain of her hopeless girlish love, the shock of having her little world turned upside down, she stared into his eyes. They were the only two people in the room. Adroitly, Nino danced her from the wide double doors into the very furthest corner, where they could not be seen. Irma surrendered herself to it, knowing full well what was on his mind. Nino stopped, flung an arm around her shoulders and kissed her, long and possessing, on the mouth. He drew away panting, his face on fire. Irma looked at him darkly. She could have killed him.

'Kiss me again!' she said defiantly, holding up her parted lips. She could feel the tears streaming down her face, dripping onto her neck, trickling across her bare shoulders.

Then they went back to join the others. They did not exchange a word. When the dancing was over and the couples began leaving the floor, Nino pulled her back.

'Will I see you tomorrow?'

'Yes.'

He spoke low and fast. 'I've got a motor boat. A racing boat. I'll pick you up in the morning. Will you come to

Chioggia with me?'

'Yes.'

'I'll be in front of the hotel at eight o'clock.'

'Eight o'clock.'

Mrs Lietzen clucked a little when she saw them both looking so red in the face.

'How can you bear to dance so long in this heat?'

'Mother,' said Irma, loudly enough for Aurelian to hear, 'Nino has kindly invited me out in his motor boat tomorrow morning. He's going to teach me to drive it.'

'I might have known!' cried Mrs Lietzen. 'You can't drive a motor car in Venice but you've found something else to make me sick with worry.'

'A boat is different,' said Mrs Lineman from behind her *pince-nez*. 'Different from a motor car. My brother has an automobile garage in Illinois…'

'Let's go home,' said Mrs Lietzen, getting to her feet. 'I'm suffocating.'

Clinging to her mother, almost in a daze, Irma went downstairs, scarcely knowing where she was going. The cool evening breeze on the Grand Canal brought her back to her senses and she realised, with a sudden little start, that she was sitting next to her mother in a motor launch, and that opposite her, in black tie and without a hat, was Aurelian, telling the driver of the *motoscafo* to go slowly because the ladies were a little over-heated.

The boat puttered tranquilly through the night, all the

way up the Grand Canal between the dark rows of *palazzi* on either side, with here and there a small patch of captive garden opening onto the water. Mrs Lietzen, muffled in her huge ermine collar, which she had turned right up so that it covered her mouth and half drowned her voice, asked,

'Are you tired, poppet?'

'No.'

'Are you in a bad mood?'

'Yes.'

'It wasn't a good party.'

'No.'

'I've had an idea!' cried Mrs Lietzen, whose mother's heart knew everything, understood everything, and whose voice sounded closer to tears than her daughter's. 'I know what we'll do. We'll rekindle the party spirit. We won't go to bed yet, but throw on some loose frock or other and settle ourselves in the big armchairs in the living-room, by the open window, enjoying the cool, night sea air, and—no gainsayers, please—we'll drink a bottle of champagne!' And then, in a voice brooking no denial, she added, 'Aurelian is invited, too.'

Aurelian was the cause of all this, she thought. And she could not bear to see her child suffer.

Irma stole a glance at Aurelian, afraid to hear him say something along the lines of, 'That's very kind, but…' She breathed freely again when all he said was,

'With pleasure. Thank you.'

They all fell silent for a while. Then suddenly a great shout went up from Mrs Lietzen.

'Oh my giddy aunt!'

Everyone assumed she had lost something again.

'We've gone past it!' she cried. 'But you can still see it... Look—there... There..!' She pointed behind them, at a house with a balcony. 'That's where they lived! Duse and D'Annunzio! Mrs Lineman was telling me about it for a whole hour yesterday.'

'And *there*,' said Aurelian, pointing at a narrow *palazzo* just two windows wide, 'is Palazzo Contarini, where Desdemona lived[19].'

Irma did not look. From somewhere inside her voluminous feather cape, which she had wrapped around her so that only her eyes peeped out, a voice made itself heard:

'I envy Desdemona.'

'Why?' asked Mrs Lietzen. 'Because Othello strangled her?'

A small, tortured voice issued from the depths of the huge feather boa.

'Exactly.'

Judith was still up and waiting for them when they got back. She was a little surprised to see Aurelian but when she heard that he was staying for an hour, she felt a quiet pleasure. Drunk and befuddled by champagne and misery,

Irma leaned out of the window and listened to the music of a serenade, floating across the water from somewhere in the distance. It was that time of night when the moonlight dances on the water and garishly dressed musicians are plucking their guitars, serenading all the foreign tourists with bogus Neapolitan folk songs. Any cultivated native Venetian who hears them is instantly possessed with a single urge: to fire a cannon into their midst. It is exactly the same feeling as a native Hungarian gets when strolling with foreign guests on the moonlit plain of the Hortobágy[20], and there, slap bang in the middle of the wilderness, he comes across a podium with a women's band dressed in red boots and hussars' waistcoats, playing all the latest ditties from Budapest. But luckily no one told Irma any of this. It was better for her not to know. The pangs of love are all the more sweetly painful when accompanied by a crooning tenor voice from across the water.

Mrs Lietzen was telling Judith about the German poet's party, with all the customary exaggeration of the duchess returning from the ball. There had been at least a hundred thousand guests. Hundreds of bulbs shining dazzlingly from the chandeliers. The ladies had been breathtakingly beautiful. Forty glittering salons had literally flowed with champagne. 'Which reminds me,' she broke off, ringing for the waiter. She ordered a bottle of champagne. It was promised directly.

'I've broken with Mrs Lineman,' she went on. 'I can't bear

the poor thing any longer. She was singing the praises of the most nauseating soup. *Zuppa di peoci*. Look it up in the dictionary. It will turn your stomach.' She shook her head with a colourful grimace. No, Mrs Lineman was no more.

'Fred and Bunny were absolutely pickled,' she went on, 'and Nino was the best-looking of all the men.' They were the words of an anxious mother, desperate to help her suffering daughter. Perhaps if she could make Aurelian jealous… She sighed. 'Oh, that Nino! It looks as though he's gone and fallen head over heels in love with Irma.' She turned to look archly at Aurelian. 'Wouldn't you say so?'

'It would hardly be surprising,' came the reply.

It satisfied Mrs Lietzen. She went to her room to get changed.

Irma turned from the window. 'And yet all Nino could talk to *me* about was Judith,' she said.

'Me?' said Judith.

'Yes. It seems you got on with him rather well. He told me you had been on a boat together.'

She was denouncing her rival for Aurelian's benefit.

'It's true,' said Judith. 'He tried to flirt with me a little. But that kind of approach doesn't work with me.'

Irma, who had turned to look out of the window again, wheeled round abruptly when she heard that. 'It sounds as though you're advertising yourself, Judith.' She looked at Aurelian, in so doing making it perfectly plain to whom she thought Judith's advertisement was being made.

It upset Aurelian to see the two women at daggers drawn. Their duelling did not inspire the smallest sense of triumph in him. He loathed it. Appeasingly, he murmured,

'Please, Irma.'

'Well, I'm sorry to say I'm not half so steadfastly, devotedly faithful to you,' said Irma, laughing. 'Nino has invited me to Chioggia with him tomorrow. On his motor boat. For the whole day. And I'm going to go. Judith would never do that.' She shot Judith a withering look.

'It's true, I wouldn't,' said Judith, meeting Irma's eyes with a level stare.

Irma laughed. 'Judith is devoted and faithful.'

Judith's head went up. She reddened.

'Oh, Judith is devoted all right.'

'Stop it,' said Aurelian. 'I can't stand any more of this.'

He went out into the corridor to smoke a cigarette but Irma took no notice. She had worked herself up into a ferment. With a forced, artificial laugh she went on,

'Because Judith wants a fat little angel. Judith wants a baby—from the person who just left the room.'

'And Judith will get one from him,' came the quiet reply. 'From the person who just left the room. And Irma would like a baby too but Irma won't get one from him.' She paused, and then added for good measure, 'From the person who just left the room.'

Irma stood staring at her for a moment in disbelief. Then she went to her room.

'Judith!' called Mrs Lietzen from her bedroom.

'I'm coming, Ma'am.'

Everyone had left the living-room. The waiter arrived with the champagne. He knocked on the door of the empty room. Then he knocked again, and then a third time, and when he still received no answer he went in and set the ice bucket down on the table. He called to Mrs Lietzen through her closed bedroom door.

'*Contessa*, your champagne. Shall I open it?'

'Yes,' replied the '*Contessa*'. 'And I shall want one, two, three, four glasses.'

'You know,' began Mrs Lietzen, turning to Judith (she had told her this before but decided to say it again now), 'there are some people who don't like being addressed as "*Contessa*" when they aren't a *Contessa*. Oh pish! say I, what does it matter that I'm not a *Contessa*? It makes me very happy to be addressed as one because it shows that I make an aristocratic sort of impression on people. He's a sweet waiter.'

The sweet waiter uncorked the champagne, dug the bottle firmly into the ice and set the glasses on the table. He was about to leave when Irma came into the room. She had followed her mother's instruction to 'throw on some loose frock or other'. She was wearing a voluminous, floor-length, diaphanous robe, made of muslin with a pattern of large flowers, fastened tightly around the waist.

'May I offer you some champagne?'

'Yes.'

It frothed up into the glass. The effects of the champagne from the German poet's party were beginning to wear off and Irma's love pangs—together with their ugly consequences—were beginning to manifest themselves again. Alcohol lasts for two hours, she thought; and then remembered an occasion when she had had the toothache, as a child, and she had been given an aspirin, and the aspirin had seemed to take all the pain away, but then two hours later her tooth had begun to throb again, so she had had to take another aspirin. My heart is beginning to throb again, she thought, and emptied her champagne glass in a single draught.

'*Brava!*' said the waiter. 'Your health!'

It was the same waiter who usually brought her breakfast in bed. He was a nice boy, with a typically Italian hooked nose. Every morning he came in to tell her that it was a fine day, ushering the good weather into the room with her morning tea. Once he had told her that he was planning to go to Mexico. He had an offer of a job in a new nightclub there.

'So tell me,' said Irma brightly, 'when is the great journey to be?'

'My ship sails in two weeks, *Contessina*.'

'Are you looking forward to it?'

'Very much. Mainly because my father is there too. He works behind the bar. It was he who got me this job. We are very close, my father and I.'

'And how is your Spanish?'

'I speak a little. But I'm swotting hard for two hours every night to improve it. It means I hardly get any sleep. But Spanish is not difficult for us Italians.'

Since Irma seemed to have no more questions, he left the room. Irma could feel the champagne beginning to take its effect, somewhere around her eyes and the region of her forehead. There is no more delightful sensation than when pain begins to subside. She lit a cigarette and leaned back in one of the big armchairs, assessing the progress of her slowly diminishing psychological toothache. It felt good to be alone. By the time Mother has finished getting changed and comes back with Judith, she told herself; by the time Aurelian has finished his cigarette, I will be myself again.

She jumped to her feet, remembering the medicines that she had seen in Judith's bedside drawer. It occurred to her that while Judith was occupied with her mother it would be as easy as anything to filch some sleeping pills. She looked at her reflection in the big console mirror.

I'm the lowest of the low, she told herself. I let Nino kiss me.

On the little table under the mirror lay her mother's evening bag, which Mrs Lietzen had thrown down there when they got in and then forgotten about. Irma opened it. How careless of Mother, she thought, seeing the brooch inside with its hazelnut-sized black pearl and the two large diamonds on either side. Anyone could have just taken it.

She smiled. She took out the brooch, then snapped her mother's bag shut and put it back where she had found it. She stood staring at the floor for some time, then slowly raised her head. Her eyes grew brighter, she began to take deep breaths. She clasped the brooch so tightly that it dug painfully into her palm. She screwed up her eyes, in the way she did when trying to focus on a distant object. Anyone could have just taken it, she said to herself again. She leaned closer to her mother's bedroom door and heard Mrs Lietzen's and Judith's voices as they debated which 'loose frock' Mrs Lietzen might put on.

'This one, do you think? Or what about the white one? No—show me the flowery one.'

She heard the sound of Judith opening and shutting the wardrobe door, and then her voice.

'Here you are. Yes—perhaps the flowery one.'

You stole it! Irma suddenly said to herself. In two strides she was by the door to the corridor, reaching for the handle.

Somebody knocked. She snatched her hand back.

'Come in.'

It was Aurelian.

'I just stepped out for a cigarette. Please excuse me. I'm a little on edge.' He looked around the room. 'Good, we're alone. There's something I want to say to you, Irma.'

Irma perched herself on the arm of one of the easy chairs. 'Well?'

'Well,' he began, 'it's—it's that I don't like strong language.

I don't like it when people make a scene. I—the only reason I didn't go home just now was because I didn't want your mother to think—well, to…'

'To what?'

'The thing is, Irma, that you won't be seeing me again. This is no way to go on. It's extremely painful for me to have to talk to you like this, especially on account of your father. And for your sake too, believe me.'

'And?'

'And—well, I can't very well explain to your parents why I shan't be seeing you again, can I? I mean, there is no need for me to justify myself, is there? It's up to you to smooth things over somehow, to think of some convincing explanation. I—I can't lie, I can't invent some sort of pretext. I—I just can't…'

'And?'

'I love Judith. I want to marry her. And for you, this… Well, I'd like you to…'

He stopped. Irma looked at him unflinchingly but at the same time a hand so cold clutched at her heart that it felt like a shaft of physical pain.

'Yes? You'd like me to what?' She pressed both hands to her chest, to try to make the pain go away, but she did so slowly and unobtrusively, so he would not guess her feelings.

'To let us disappear from your lives, quite naturally, without any fuss and palaver. Don't be unkind to us. I am going to ask Judith to leave your family's service tomorrow.

I can't bear the idea of you—of her having to… Not for a single day longer… But out of respect for your mother, for the half-hour that's left of this evening, I'll—I'll…'

'Grin and bear it?'

'I'll grin and bear it.'

Like someone who has just struck a deal, Irma held out her hand. It was a last plea for alms, the kind of humiliating supplication that only lovers who have experienced it can really understand. There was no reason for them to shake hands otherwise. She just wanted to feel his hand in hers one last time. She no longer expected any spark of electricity from his eyes. His eyes had lost their power. Some kind of cruel short circuit had robbed Aurelian's gaze of its electric charge. Once again, this is something that only lovers truly know how to detect, that moment when the very last flicker of interest finally sputters out in the eyes of the other. There is no mistaking it when it happens.

They shook hands.

'I'd like a cigarette please,' said Irma.

Aurelian lit one for her and then took one himself. Irma handed him a glass of champagne.

'Cheers!' She raised her glass and took a small sip. 'Would you excuse me for a moment?'

She went to her room. Aurelian breathed a sigh of relief.

Irma did not linger in her bedroom; she made straight for the door that led into the long, red-carpeted corridor. Seeing that no one was about, she softly closed her bedroom door and stole along the corridor to Judith's room. The key was in the lock. She went in and turned on the light. Closing the door behind her, she thought, if Judith comes in and finds me here, I'll say I've come to look for a sleeping draught. She lifted the lid of Judith's big green trunk, scrabbled to make a small space amid all the things that were crammed in one corner, and buried the brooch—the hazelnut-sized pearl with its accompanying diamonds—deep down among them. Then she closed the trunk, switched off the light and went back to her room the way she had come.

'Someone has stolen it!' he said, almost out loud. She stopped to listen. No sound came from the living-room. But then a few moments later she heard her mother coming in with Judith and asking,

'Where's Irma?'

'In her room,' Aurelian replied.

'I'm just coming!' Irma called out. She stood leaning against her bedroom wall, composing herself. Now she well and truly *had* pushed Judith into the canal! Not like the other night, on the bridge. This time she had really done it. And she felt completely hollow inside, unable to distinguish good from bad. She was not angry, she was not upset, she was not in pain, she did not feel like crying. She did not feel like laughing either. Was she awake? Was she asleep? Did she want to live? Or die? She did not care. She felt nothing at all except nothingness itself. What ineffable calm!

It was enveloped in this new sensation that she went

back into the living-room, to be greeted by a question from her mother.

'Well, poppet? Are we having a drink or aren't we?'

'We certainly are!' Irma replied, draining the last drop from her champagne glass.

Half an hour later Mrs Lietzen got to her feet.

'I'm exhausted,' she said. 'This evening has done me in. You young people carry on if you feel like it. I'm going to bed.'

Mrs Lietzen did not normally say things like that. Irma was usually expected to go to bed at the same time as her mother. But today Mrs Lietzen felt so deeply moved by the plight of her woebegone, lovelorn little girl that she would have done anything in her power not to cause her pain. It was not true that she was exhausted. She knew full well that sleep would elude her and that she would lie tossing and turning for hours. But she had a keen sense of being in the way and she knew that all her solicitude just made things worse for her poor, suffering daughter.

'Come along, Judith dear,' she said. 'I'll need you to give me my little injection. Then you can go back and join them.' She looked across at Irma, hoping to see a sign of gratitude, but Irma was not looking at her. To get her attention, she said, 'Irma, dear!'

The eyes that Irma turned on her mother were completely devoid of expression and open a little too wide.

'Irma, dear,' Mrs Lietzen said again, 'I just want to remind you not to stay up too late. You've got to get up very early tomorrow, remember, if you want to go out with Nino in the motor boat…'

'I'll just finish this cigarette and have a tiny drop more champagne.'

'All right, poppet. Night-night.'

She collected her evening bag from the console table and left the room with Judith.

The process of getting her into her nightclothes and administering the injection took rather a long time. Irma did not say a word to Aurelian while it was going on, nor did she look once in his direction. She smoked her cigarette slowly, taking small sips from her half-glass of champagne. They sat together in total silence until Judith came back.

'I think I'll turn in,' Judith said.

Aurelian got to his feet. He held out a hand to Irma.

'It's time I was on my way too.'

'So, this is where we say farewell,' said Irma. She stood up, shook his hand and then disappeared into her bedroom.

Aurelian and Judith left the room as well. They went out in the corridor. When the Lietzen apartment was a good few paces behind them, they stopped.

'I told her,' Aurelian said. 'I told her I wouldn't be coming here again.'

Judith had begun to cry quietly. 'I can't stay here. I can't bear to be with them. It's awful. I've got to get away.'

'Don't cry,' Aurelian said. 'Oh my darling, please don't

cry.'

His words had the effect of making Judith cry even harder. 'Don't leave me!' she begged him. She went to her room and opened the door, using her other hand to rub her eyes. She was sobbing convulsively.

'Darling,' Aurelian said. 'My darling…'

'Don't leave me!'

'You mustn't talk like this.'

The door was wide open. Judith had sunk onto the chair in front of her desk. Her body was racked with sobs. Aurelian stood in the doorway.

'Don't leave me alone here!'

'I told her that *you* would be leaving them tomorrow, too,' Aurelian said. 'Without fail.'

'Without fail!' sobbed Judith. 'Tomorrow morning!'

'I won't let you put up with… Not for a minute longer— not even the smallest… I mean, your position…'

He was getting himself worked up. He took two steps into the room as he spoke. The door was still wide open.

'But how am I to do it?' asked Judith, turning her tear-stained face to his, beseechingly.

'I think you should just leave, as simply as that. If you start trying to explain things to Mrs Lietzen you'll find yourself tied up in knots and everything will get awkward. And you'll find yourself having to deal with Irma again, too. If I were you, I would leave a letter for Mrs Lietzen, short and to the point, saying that…'—he turned and closed the door—'…saying that you are no longer able to tolerate the tone that Irma takes with you, nor the distinctly hostile atmosphere in which you…'

Judith held up a hand. 'Just a minute, my love…' She picked up a pencil. 'How did you express it again? Tolerate the tone…?'

Aurelian began to dictate. '…that Irma takes with me…'

'…takes with me…'

'Nor the distinctly hostile atmosphere…which every minute of the day…'

Judith wrote down everything he said, word for word. Then she looked up.

'And where should I go tomorrow morning?'

'Leave that to me. I'll sort it out with the help of my concierge. First thing tomorrow morning I'll send you a message telling you which *pensione* I've booked a room in. And then, calmly and sensibly, we can discuss what happens next.'

Judith went over to him and put her arms around his neck. Her gesture was almost maternal. She turned her pale face to his. 'We must make sure to be happy,' she said. 'Happy forever once this is over.'

They kissed, filled with a mixture of rapture and relief. Then Aurelian turned to go. From the doorway he whispered, 'I'll send word in the morning, first thing.'

And he was gone.

Judith dried her eyes. She sat for a while deep in thought,

her elbows on the desk, on the little velour mat. Then she sighed, stood up and threw open her wardrobe door. It was time to start packing. Her eyes travelled over the piles of linen, the dresses hanging in the cupboard. She dragged out her trunk and propped open the lid, then looked back at all the things in the wardrobe. Her worry was the worry that besets all packers: How is it all going to fit in? She began to remove armfuls of her belongings from the trunk, emptying it all out onto the dressing table.

From beneath the folds of a thick grey winter scarf, the twin diamonds flanking the black pearl winked up at her. Judith stared at them and froze.

What did this mean? She was seized with sudden panic. She sat down at the desk once more, burying her head in her hands, waiting for her thudding heart to subside. Then she went over to the trunk again and looked at the familiar, winking jewel.

'But I don't understand it. I don't understand!' she said out loud.

Her heartbeat refused to subside.

'What am I to do?'

She pressed a hand to her eyes. Then, seized with resolution, she snatched up the brooch, left her room without bothering to shut the door and made her way straight to Mrs Lietzen's bedroom. Very softly, she knocked.

'Who is it?' asked a wary voice.

'It's Judith, Ma'am.'

'Come in.'

The light was on. Mrs Lietzen was reading in bed. Judith approached, brooch in hand, and held it out under the bedside lamp.

'Gracious Heavens!' cried Mrs Lietzen, raising herself up on her elbows. 'Where did this come from?' She took the brooch from Judith's hand.

'It's the most terrible thing,' Judith said. 'I found it in my travelling trunk.'

Mrs Lietzen gasped. She pointed towards the dressing table. 'Hand me my evening bag.'

Judith did so and Mrs Lietzen opened it with trembling fingers, as if the brooch that she held in her other hand could possibly still be inside.

'The clasp came undone during the *soirée*,' she said, sinking stupidly back against her pillows. 'It fell off and someone found it and then I put it in my evening bag. I was going to take it to a jeweller to get it mended. And now what's this you tell me? Where did you find it?'

'In my travelling trunk. Wedged into a corner at the bottom, buried under my winter scarf.'

'All right, let's work backwards. When we got home, I put my bag down on the console table in the living-room. That's where it was when I collected it before coming to bed. So in the meantime, someone must have taken the brooch. But how did it find its way into your travelling trunk?'

'I don't know.'

'There are thieves in the hotel,' Mrs Lietzen declared. Sitting up straight, she reached an unsteady hand towards the telephone and picked up the receiver. 'I wish to speak to the manager.'

Judith looked at her watch. 'It's almost two o'clock,' she said softly.

'I don't care if it's almost twenty o'clock,' said Mrs Lietzen in ringing tones. 'I still wish to speak to the manager.'

She sank back against her pile of pillows once more, all colour drained from her cheeks. With the brooch tightly clasped in one hand, she composed herself to wait for the manager. At last they heard his knock.

'Come in.'

'What is the matter?' the hotel manager asked, coming to stand by Mrs Lietzen's bed, his face the face of a doctor awakened from his night's sleep, sympathetic and reassuring.

Calmly, quietly and precisely, not stirring from her pillows, Mrs Lietzen described the state of affairs. When she had finished, as if to prove the veracity of her tale, she opened her hand and presented the great brooch to the manager's gaze, all the while looking at him meaningfully.

The hotel manager was flustered. 'We must stay calm,' he said. 'I implore you to stay calm.'

The words were spoken entirely for his own benefit since neither of the two women had moved a hair. He turned to Judith.

'You found it in your trunk just now, Miss?'

'Yes. Ten minutes ago.'

'When did you go to your room?'

'Half an hour ago.'

'And until that time, your door was locked?'

'No. The key was in the lock on the outside.'

'Oh, but come, come!' the manager spluttered, spreading his hands, 'If ladies will not lock their doors when they leave their rooms...'

'Then pieces of my jewellery, of their own accord, will make their way from my suite to Room 120, is that it?' said Mrs Lietzen with asperity.

The manager turned to Judith again. 'Did anyone go into your room while you were out?'

'Not to my knowledge.'

'And from the time you went back to your room until the moment you discovered the brooch, was anyone with you in your room?'

'Nobody,' Judith told him.

Irma, still fully dressed, was lying on her bed in the dark, staring out at the sky through the open window. She was conscious of nothing at all except that her eyes seemed wider open than usual and that she found it difficult to close her lids. The full moon was shining on her face.

'Two francs,' she mumbled to herself.

That spring, in Cannes, they had stood looking at the full moon from the waterfront, where a garrulous little man had set up a tripod telescope, trained on the sky, hoping to tempt gamblers on their way to the casino with close-up views of the moon and of Jupiter. The Lietzens had fallen for his patter. First they had looked at the terrible great rugged silver orb that is the moon, then turned the telescope to pick out tiny Jupiter, about the size of a cufflink.

'How much do we owe you?' Father had asked.

'Three francs,' had come the star-merchant's reply. 'Two for the moon and one for Jupiter.'

'Two francs,' mumbled Irma to the moon, staring hard at its pallid disc with her wide-open eyes.

She lay staring at it for a long time, motionless, until suddenly loud music began blaring across the lagoon. A saxophone solo, tinny and mournful and adenoidal. Her eyes left the moon. She went over to the window and looked out at the water. A huge, brightly lit rectangular raft was drifting slowly and languidly along, heading out to sea, riding high in the water and crammed with a long dining table and a group of people in dinner jackets and ball gowns, partying noisily, some of them sitting round the table while others were taking turns on a gleaming parquet dance floor. The music, the lights and the laughter punched shrill holes in the night. This was the *Galleggiante*, the Moorish-style pleasure raft belonging to the Excelsior, the luxury hotel on the Lido. Every night it plied its way up and down the Grand Canal while its consignment of customers drank and danced and made merry. Far up in front, so far away that it could scarcely be seen, attached to it by a length of rope, was a little tugboat, gamely pulling it along, but at a discreet distance so that the revellers on board could neither see nor hear the grimy, smoky, chugging engine that was in fact their means of propulsion. With its bright electric lights provided by hidden generators; with its white tablecloths, its gaggle of merrymakers and its scurrying waiters, this gay and garish spectacle, floating along on the black water, seemed to Irma from her high window like the illuminated dining-room of a grand seaside hotel that had somehow detached itself from its surroundings and floated off into the night. And it was floating further and further away, sparkling on the water as it went, ablaze with glimmering lights and colourful bunting. And there she was too, and so was everyone she knew, her parents, all her rich friends, their entire contented, well-to-do world, all dressed in their dinner jackets, the women semi-clad in brightly shimmering silk, amid the brassy breaths of the saxophone's lament, the champagne and the flowers, enjoying one last, mad hurrah on a raft of the dead that was slowly gliding further and further from the shore, laden with a cargo of laughter and lights, heading steadily out across the silent water, bound for the cold, black ocean that was the world beyond, on whose distant shore, far, far away, cold, black demons were massing, in silent anticipation of their arrival...

Sleep finally claimed her, in her armchair. She slept for a couple of hours, to be woken at seven by the sun shining full on her face. She dressed and went to the window. Nino was standing on the quay in a leather jacket and cap. He raised an arm in salute.

Irma tiptoed out of her room. The hotel was still slumbering. When she got down to the quay, Nino handed her a leather jacket like his, and jammed a leather cap on her head. He helped her aboard the motor boat, then sat down at the wheel.

In her leather jacket, under the warm morning sun, Irma shivered. In a high, thin little voice, feigning a brightness she did not feel, she said to Nino,

'Not that I'm afraid of the sea or anything, but please don't bring me home until the evening. However much I might beg you otherwise.'

'Trust me,' laughed Nino.

Behind them the water abruptly began to boil. The bow of the motor boat reared high above the surface, as if it was trying to fly, and then, with a howl of protest, shot forward across the lagoon. It was a perfect summer's morning, fresh and warm, without a single cloud in the blue sky.

10

A little later that same morning, Mrs Lietzen picked up the telephone and summoned Judith to her bedroom. Judith took with her the letter that Aurelian had dictated and which contained the reasons for her planned sudden departure. But she did not give it to Mrs Lietzen. After all that had happened, she realised, there could be no question of a sudden departure. There were other things that had to be sorted out first.

At the same time as Judith was knocking on Mrs Lietzen's door, Irma was racing past San Servolo, the asylum island, where the unfortunate inmates stare out at the blue water through the bars of their cells.

Judith found Mrs Lietzen sitting enthroned against a mass of pillows in her majestic black and gold bed, looking for all the world like a latter-day Maria Theresa. In fact, she was feeling rather like Maria Theresa. A different waiter, a young boy with blonde hair, had just brought her her breakfast. Mrs Lietzen addressed him in French.

'Where is the other waiter, the one who usually serves us in our rooms?'

'He's downstairs in the office, Ma'am. He's being interrogated.'

'Who by?'

'A—a detective.'

Mrs Lietzen put down the teapot. 'So *he* did it?'

'They'll pin it on him, Ma'am. I mean, the detective will.'

'And what is the evidence against him?'

'There isn't any. They just say that logically it must have been him because he was the only person who came up to your suite, and he was alone here with the bag for a few minutes, and all of us waiters have keys to every room.'

Mrs Lietzen shook her head as if there was something she did not understand. 'But why should he have hidden it in *Mademoiselle's* travelling trunk, in amongst all her things?'

The waiter looked uncomfortable. He did not enjoy repeating the accusations that were being made against his colleague.

'He said—I mean, the man from the police said, that what always happens in hotels, if something goes missing, is that the staff quarters are the first places to be searched. So apparently what the thieves do is hide the stuff in one of the guest's bedrooms, because no one ever searches there. And then when everything has died down, the thief goes back and retrieves the swag. Poor devil! He was just about to set off for Mexico to join his father.'

'That makes it all the more likely to be him,' said Mrs Lietzen.

The waiter felt very sorry indeed for his poor, hook-nosed colleague. 'This might have ruined his life,' he said.

And then, very quietly and respectfully, he added, 'The *Contessa* could change that, though... Just a few words would do it.'

From amongst her pillows the *Contessa* gave a little yelp. 'Oh, just leave me in peace! How could I possibly change anything?'

Timidly, the waiter said, 'I only dared to think that perhaps—that maybe...'

The *Contessa* began to whimper and blocked her ears. 'Leave me in peace, I tell you! There is nothing I can do. Just go, all of you. Leave me in peace!' The second 'in peace' came out as a rather melodramatic scream.

Judith, who up until then had been standing at the window in silence, went over to the waiter and gently signalled that he should leave the room. White-haired Mrs Lietzen lay groaning in bed like a patient at death's door.

'I don't want to hear any more about it,' she moaned. 'They can murder each other for all I care. Just leave me in peace!'

Mrs Lietzen's nature, in common with that of so many women of her type, was a mixture of lofty abstraction and down-to-earth practicality. The trouble was that no one knew which characteristic she would choose to deploy at any given time. Once, in church, a friend kneeling beside her had turned to her in the pew and whispered, 'Well, that's put paid to my twenty-*pengő*[21] silk stockings! I can just tell I've torn a ladder in them.' To which Mrs Lietzen had replied,

'Well, quite. That's why one puts on a pair of four-*pengő*-fifty stockings when one knows there's going to be a hassock involved.' When faced with genuine danger, however, her practical side deserted her. Once, in Budapest, she had been driving across Calvin Square when she suddenly realised that trams were bearing down on her from three directions at the same time. Realising that only the good Lord could save her, she had screamed and let go of the steering wheel, clasping her hands together in frantic prayer.

'A weak and feeble woman,' she whimpered now, 'left all alone in a situation like this! Completely alone!'

'Shall I send for Mrs Lineman?' asked Judith tentatively.

'Saints preserve us, no!' Mrs Lietzen dragged herself into a sitting position. 'What we need is a man! Judith, I want you immediately to put a call through to the bank. Ask them to tell Aurelian Szabó to drop everything and come here at once.'

Somewhat reluctantly, Judith went through to the living-room to make the call. She could have telephoned Aurelian some time ago, at his lodgings, but she had not wanted to disturb or alarm him—for no real reason, as she saw it. She returned to Mrs Lietzen.

'He is on his way. And the hotel manager is waiting in the living-room. May I show him in?'

'Just a moment. Give me the mirror and my face powder.'

Mrs Lietzen shrugged herself into a black silk bedjacket embroidered with golden storks and jammed her rings onto her fingers. She almost put on the red hat. Then she plumped up the pillows and leaned back, signalling like a languid Maria Theresa to her lady-in-waiting that she would receive the chancellor now.

The manager came in, grinned intensely and then immediately lost all facial expression, as was his wont. He was very tactful and circumspect but surely *Madame* must understand (as far as the manager was concerned, Mrs Lietzen was never '*Contessa*') that for the sake of the hotel's good name, this must all be properly cleared up? He could not simply allow his staff to go around being suspected of theft. He had the hotel's international reputation to think of. The crowned heads of the whole of Scandinavia came here every year; the old King of Sweden for the tennis tournament on the Lido, the King of Denmark for the sailing races…

'And the King of Norway?' Mrs Lietzen cut in sarcastically.

'He—His Highness has not yet done us the honour.'

'How disappointing.'

'Please, *Madame*, spare me your gibes,' protested the manager. 'This whole affair touches me very nearly. I must find a way to have it cleared up fairly and squarely because if it is not—well, there will be talk. Gossip about us will spread from Stockholm to New York.'

There is no point upon which grand hotels are so sensitive as on the subject of jewellery. A single word is all that would be required, just one single whispered insinuation, for the bejewelled ladies of North America to start avoiding an establishment like the plague. Heaven forbid!

'I have had to involve the police in the investigation,' the manager went on, 'because it is my sincere conviction that my staff are innocent.'

'But have the police not also come to the conclusion that your waiter is the culprit?' said Mrs Lietzen with asperity.

'Oh, the primitive mind of the police inspector!' cried the manager. 'That is precisely why I made so bold as to come here, *Madame*, to ask if you would be so good as to allow the gentleman from the police department to talk to you, just for a moment or two, to clarify one or two points.'

'Of course. Show him up.'

The manager went into the living-room to telephone his office.

'I daresay it will turn out that I stole my brooch myself,' muttered Mrs Lietzen. She looked about her to see what else she could put on to impress the police inspector, but found nothing.

The manager came back.

'He will be here directly. It is of the utmost importance that the hotel's name should be cleared…'

'Yes, yes,' cut in Mrs Lietzen, waving her hand dismissively in her best Maria Theresa manner.

There was silence while they waited. In order to fill the time, Judith asked the manager,

'You do not suspect the waiter, then?'

'No. My suspicions take me in a different direction.'

Though he was replying to Judith's question, he looked at Mrs Lietzen as he spoke, thereby making it clear that his reason for not looking at Judith was deliberate. Judith's breath caught in her throat.

There was a knock at the door and the 'gentleman from the police department', as the manager called him (pointedly avoiding the word 'detective'), came in. As soon as Mrs Lietzen saw him, she suppressed a smile. He could not be anything other than what he was. The foreigner abroad might mistake a uniformed policeman for a soldier or a fireman, but the plain clothes policeman is unmistakable everywhere he goes.

The gentleman from the police department got straight to the point.

'May I see the article in question, please?'

Maria Theresa stretched out a languorous, imperial hand and picked up her bag from where it lay on top of her bedside table. She opened it, looked inside and then let out a scream. It was not the voice of Maria Theresa; it was the voice of Mrs Stephen Lietzen, née Hermina Kovács, that squeaked, 'It's gone!'

But as soon as she had uttered them, she waved her words aside. 'Oh, but of course, how stupid of me! I put it back in its box. Take it out again, would you, Judith? Gracious, what a turn I gave myself!'

The detective, when he was handed the brooch, looked at it through narrowed eyes, as if subjecting it to interrogation. The two large diamonds stared back at him with cold insolence.

'Value?'

'Hundreds of thousands!' said Maria Theresa.

'Is it insured?'

'Of course,' snapped Hermina.

The detective handed it back, holding it aloft between thumb and forefinger, as if to say, 'As you are my witnesses, I have returned it.' Then he turned to Judith.

'When did you find it?'

'At half past one in the morning.'

'And did you bring it here straight away?'

'Yes.'

'And where did you find it? Be precise, please.'

'At the bottom of my travelling trunk.'

'And why were you rummaging around in your travelling trunk at half past one in the morning?'

Judith noticed that the hotel manager was nodding in approbation. It was clear that he had already steered the detective's suspicions in a certain direction.

'I was packing.'

The hotel manager immediately turned to Mrs Lietzen.

'Is *Madame* leaving us?'

'No.'

'I was under the impression that you were staying for several more weeks.'

'We are.'

The detective crossed the logical bridge that the hotel manager had just constructed for him.

'So why were you packing your things at half past one in the morning?'

Judith could just as well have said that she was tidying something away. But she sensed danger, and since she was innocent, she thought the best thing to do was to tell the truth.

'I was planning to move out.'

'At dead of night?'

'No. First thing this morning.'

Mrs Lietzen sat bolt upright. 'I knew nothing about this!'

Slowly and deliberately, the gentleman from the police department asked, 'Why did you want to move out, first thing this morning, without your mistress's knowledge?'

Judith said nothing for a few moments. Then, very firmly, she said, 'That has no bearing on the matter.'

As soon as she had said it, it came to her in a flash that it was Irma who had taken the brooch. Irma was the thief! But no—why? And yet she was sure of it.

The hotel manager no longer took the trouble to disguise his opinion. He looked scornfully from Judith to the detective. Judith felt a little of her calm begin to desert her.

'Please,' she said, 'there is no need for any of this. We have the brooch, we have not lodged a complaint, there is no reason to create a scandal. And certainly no reason to make a fuss. For *Madame*'s sake.'

'I beg your pardon,' the hotel manager said, holding up his hand, 'but you are mistaken. It is not for you to decide the extent to which we make a fuss.'

Mrs Lietzen had still not recovered from the first shock. From the bed, her perplexed voice said in Hungarian,

'But Judith, why did you want to run away first thing this morning?'

'Run away? I didn't want to run away. I wanted to leave.'

'As far as I am concerned,' was Mrs Lietzen's peremptory rejoinder, 'if you leave my household without my knowledge it comes to the same thing. It's running away,'.

Judith began to get flustered. 'Here,' she said, taking out the letter, 'here are my reasons. I planned to leave you this letter. I didn't have the chance to do so earlier. But here it is now.'

She handed the letter to Mrs Lietzen. The two men waited in respectful silence as the flow of incomprehensible Hungarian dialogue passed over them. So now a letter had cropped up. And there was clearly some kind of tension between the two women. The hotel manager nudged the detective in the ribs. They waited while Mrs Lietzen read the letter and then looked at Judith.

'Clearly, as things stand,' Judith said, 'I can't just leave you here all by yourself. But as soon as Irma gets back I'll go.'

Mrs Lietzen slowly let the letter fall onto the counterpane. The gentleman from the police department summed up the facts as they stood.

'It is obvious that someone took the brooch into the young lady's room and hid it there. It's a classic trick with jewel thieves. They don't steal the item as such, they just *transplant* it. The same technique is used in jewellers' shops. The thief will be looking through a tray of objects and then he'll stick one under the tabletop with a lump of wax. Whatever happens next, the object won't be found about his person. And then, perhaps about a month later, a lady accomplice will go to the shop, look through a tray of jewels, and nimbly detach the item that is stuck under the table. So far so good. But there are still one or two things I'd like to know about that waiter who is planning to go to Mexico...'

The detective's summary contained nothing that the hotel manager did not know already. He was beginning to think he was being personally slighted.

'It won't make any difference how many times you ask about him. I'll keep telling you the same thing.'

'But I have a different question this time,' the detective said. 'Are the apartments next to the *bella signorina*'s room occupied?'

Bella signorina! It was a policeman's way of softening the blow to the accused. The hotel manager perked up.

'I have already looked into that. One of the adjacent rooms is empty. The other is occupied by the valet of a Spanish *señor*. The ones on the other side are servants' quarters.' Just so long as the detective did not go thinking that the *bella signorina* was a lady...

The two men went off to find the Spanish *señor*'s valet. Mrs Lietzen sank back against her pillows, greatly struck by the hotel manager's idea—which was easy to decipher because it was so simple, even glaringly obvious. The family nurse, on the point of leaving her employer, stole the brooch, then took fright, repented, and brought it back.

They waited in silence for a long time. It seemed that the Spanish *señor*'s valet had had something to impart. At length, without looking at Judith, Mrs Lietzen said,

'You were planning to leave this morning?'

'Yes.'

'But why so suddenly, without giving in your notice? What's behind it all?'

There was a short silence. Then Judith said,

'I'm going to get married.'

'To whom?'

'To someone who lives here.'

Mrs Lietzen said nothing further. She knew who Judith was referring to, there was no need to spell it out. They relapsed into silence. Mrs Lietzen quite saw how impossible it had become for Judith to stay with them for a single day longer. She suppressed a heavy sigh. She was thinking of her daughter.

At last the gentleman from the police department came back with the hotel manager. The detective's demeanour was unchanged but the manager's face was bright with an unmistakable glow of triumph.

'The Spanish *señor*'s valet tells us that he heard voices coming from your room,' said the detective. 'There was a heated discussion going on. Someone was crying.'

For good measure, the hotel manager added, 'After midnight, between one and two in the morning.'

A cold hand of fear now clutched at Judith's heart. They would end up dragging Aurelian into all this. No, she told herself, that could not happen. I will not let it happen. Over my dead body. She forced herself to meet the detective's eyes.

'So,' he said, 'it seems that there *was* somebody in your room after all. And yet you told us that no one was with you.'

'No one was with me.'

'Why do you not confess? Perhaps that person had the brooch with him and hid it in your trunk, without your knowledge.' When Judith greeted this remark with silence, he added, 'Or *with* your knowledge.' He shrugged and spread his hands, then dropped them again, so that they slapped dully against his thighs. 'You did a noble thing,' he went on. 'You acted perfectly correctly, because when this person left, you took fright and gave back the brooch. We have seen this kind of thing happen before. It is not unusual and it is absolutely the correct way to behave. You wanted to put everything right. But now you must tell us who it was who was with you.'

'No one. Nobody was with me.'

'But voices were heard in your room. And somebody was crying.'

'Yes. I was crying.'

The gentleman from the police department had finally reached the limits of his patience. 'In that case it was you who stole the brooch.'

Judith dropped her eyes.

The detective continued. 'Your hotel manager is a good psychologist. You stole the brooch, you repented of the deed, you gave it back. Straight away, before it was missed, in the middle of the night. No harm has been done but nevertheless a theft was committed and the hotel waiter was not the culprit.'

'No,' said the hotel manager, quietly but forcefully. 'And I should very much like that to be officially stated in the police report.'

Mrs Lietzen stared at the ceiling with its carved wooden coffers, regular sky-blue squares with a gold rosette between each one.

'I am sorry, *Signorina*, but I must ask you to accompany me to the *Questura*. Just a formality, but we must file a detailed report.'

The hotel manager turned to Mrs Lietzen and said, very quietly, 'For us, this kind of thing… That is to say, this kind of thing is of national importance. A thousand pardons, *Madame*, but the Venetian tourist industry, after all… Millions have been invested in these hotels…'

'And the truth is important, too,' the gentleman from the police department put in.

Judith turned towards the bed and said, 'Please help me, Ma'am. I can't let myself be taken off by the police like this!'

A weak little voice was heard from somewhere among the pillows.

'Where is Irma?'

'She has gone out for the day.'

The white-haired lady began weeping soundlessly. 'There's nothing I can possibly do,' she snivelled. 'I don't understand any of this.'

Once again, like that time in Calvin Square, she had let go of the steering wheel.

'I feel faint,' she faltered.

Judith, white as a sheet, went to fetch a glass of water. She stirred some powder into it with a spoon. With her left hand she raised Mrs Lietzen's drooping head and put the spoon to her lips. Then she opened a lavender-coloured velvet pouch and took out a syringe. Silently, tactfully, the two men left the room. They waited in the living-room until Judith had finished what she had to do. Judith made to go after them and turned to close the bedroom door.

'No!' came the voice from the bed. 'Leave the door open. I want to hear everything that happens.'

Judith opened the door wide. Just at that moment the other door to the living-room opened and Aurelian came in. As he did so, he heard the sound of a man sobbing in the corridor. The unfortunate hook-nosed waiter was waiting outside with the other detective, who said,

'Aren't you ashamed of yourself? A grown man, blubbing like that?'

'I—I've got my ticket. To...'

The door closed on the word 'Mexico'. Judith inclined her head in the direction of Mrs Lietzen's room and said,

'She's feeling poorly.'

'What are you all whispering about?' came a tetchy voice from the bed, as the two men informed Aurelian of what had happened.

'My respects, Ma'am,' Aurelian said, presenting himself in Mrs Lietzen's doorway. 'I'm here. You sent for me.' And then, appalled and aghast, he turned back to the two men in the living-room.

The silence was broken only by the sounds of the hook-nosed waiter's sobs on the far side of the door.

'The waiter is innocent,' said the hotel manager, 'I'm convinced of it. The *Signorina* can tell us the truth. I am sure she will speak more freely when she gets to the *Questura*. There is someone she is shielding, someone who was with her last night. When we get her to the police station we will find out the identity of this late-night caller and she will no doubt tell us what she was discussing with him so urgently and why she was crying. The boy in the next-door room heard it all. It's true that he is only a valet but he isn't deaf and nor is he a liar.'

With that, the manager went out to tell the hook-nosed waiter to stop making such a noise in the hotel corridor. The gentleman from the police department turned to Judith.

'Please get your coat and come with me, *Signorina*. The waiter is waiting for me outside. It is time we were on our way.'

Aurelian stared at Judith, who had found her hat, in preparation for departure. He turned to the unknown man.

'Are you a detective?'

'Yes.'

Aurelian looked at him squarely. 'It was me. I am the person who was in the *Signorina*'s room last night.' He took a card out of his wallet and gave it to the policeman.

A stifled gasp came from Mrs Lietzen's bedroom. It was followed by a tense, inquisitive silence.

Aurelian ignored the gasp. He did not so much as turn round. 'I was there for about a quarter of an hour. I was dictating a letter to the *Signorina*.'

The detective looked at the name card. 'Dictating a letter. Thank you. And might I enquire whether you have been here before? In the room we are standing in now, I mean?'

'Yes. It was from this room that I took my leave last night. And then, on my way out, I stopped in the *Signorina*'s room.'

'Thank you. Please be so good as to come with us. *Signorina*,' he added significantly, 'I think it highly likely that within half an hour you will be back here again. Now, let us be on our way.'

Aurelian took Judith's hand.

'Not like that,' the detective said sharply. 'One by one,

please. You are to follow me in single file.'

Out in the corridor they split up. The second detective went ahead with Aurelian and the hook-nosed waiter. The first detective accompanied Judith down the stairs and then across the lobby, moving slowly so as not to attract the slightest attention. Fred was there in his travelling clothes and hat, with a camera slung over his shoulder. Wreathed in smiles, he was distributing tips to the porters and bell boys, who were standing round him in a swarm. Outside, in front of the revolving doors, with a coat draped across her arm and a large jewellery case in her hand, stood Bunny, waiting for him, ready to leave. Pretty as a picture, she stood guarding the gondola that was piled high with their luggage. The brand new, soft yellow pigskin cases, redolent of a pair of British lives about to begin in earnest, were already embossed with their first brightly coloured hotel sticker.

In the tranquil lagoon, a little way off from the Lido shore, the speedboat had come to a standstill. Viewed from any of the distant sailing boats, which were likewise completely becalmed, the only thing that could be made out was a bulky leather jacket with another, smaller leather jacket sitting motionlessly beside it. Malamocco was visible on the skyline. It had taken them about half an hour to get this far, tearing across the water. Luckily the motor boat had made such a noise that there had been no need to speak as they roared along. Irma stared blankly into space. She felt as though an invisible, retributory force was pulling her forward, dragging her away from her own life. It seemed to be trying to cry out to her from the far shore, clamorous with things it wanted to tell her, but the terrible, all-encompassing, all-obliterating roar of the engine was drowning out all sound. At last, Irma could bear it no longer. She asked Nino to stop the boat. He cut the engine.

'But we aren't even halfway there,' he protested.

'Take me back,' said Irma.

'No fear!' laughed Nino. 'You told me not to take you back, not even…'

'Take me back!' Irma shouted, so peremptorily and so coldly that Nino just stared at her. 'If you don't take me back this instant…' She stood to her feet. 'Take me back, do you hear?'

It was the kind of female voice that drains the last drop of enjoyment out of everything for a man.

'As you wish,' said Nino. He started the engine and turned the boat in a wide semicircle, pointing it back the way they had come.

Irma sensed that she had offended this decent, well-mannered fellow, who had never done anything to hurt her. Burying herself in the large jacket she tried to make excuses for her conduct.

'My mother is not well. I'm worried about her.'

The motor boat put on a burst of speed. Irma could see from Nino's face that her behaviour had bruised him badly.

She shouted to be heard above the roar of the engine.

'I'll just look in on her quickly and then we'll go for lunch together on the Lido.'

Nino nodded but his face was stony. He stopped the boat in front of the hotel, tying it up to the broad quay. He jumped ashore and helped Irma to disembark. She had shed her leather jacket and now stood smiling at him, grimly flirtatious.

'Wait here.'

'As you wish,' said Nino politely. He looked after her as she went through the revolving door. He liked this girl a lot. He settled down to wait.

As soon as she was in the lobby, Irma found herself face to face with the hotel manager, who treated her to a radiant smile, his face performing its usual trick of snapping back out of its smirk into expressionlessness again, as rapidly as an elastic band that one stretches and then lets go. Irma stopped, looking at him interrogatively.

'There has been a theft,' the manager told her, 'but the item has been retrieved. It was the nurse who did it.'

'And?'

'The police have taken her away.'

11

Irma went upstairs. She did not stop to look in on her mother. She went straight down the corridor to her own room, then stopped at the door into the living-room and listened. There was complete silence. She took a step forward, thinking that she had better go to her mother, but then stopped again. She did not have the courage. She would go presently, in a little while. For now she just needed to… What exactly? She just needed… It was difficult to say. She threw herself on the bed. She needed to think. What had the manager said? Judith had been taken away by the police. I deserve to be shot on the spot, like a stray dog, she thought. Her mind began to race. I wasn't drunk when I did it, she told herself. It would be lying to say that I was. It wouldn't be true. And then a childish excuse occurred to her. It wasn't evil, what I did, it wasn't done out of spite. It was a crime of passion. But then a little voice whispered, 'You pushed her into the canal.' And immediately afterwards she had a sense of something she could not put into words; it was just a very clear feeling: when she had done what she did, it had not been the *result* that had mattered, it was the *gesture*. The gesture had been an end in itself. It was exactly the same when she had almost pushed Judith off the bridge. If she had actually succeeded in doing so, she would never have lived it down. But the flash of satisfaction she had felt at giving Judith that physical shove: that was something she had irresistibly needed to feel. It was like when people say, 'I could have killed her,' except that in Irma's case the mad impulse had taken her one stage further. She really *had* been able to make as if to kill her opponent, because she had wanted to know what it felt like. To *feel* it, that was the thing. But no more than that. It was a kind of idealised desire, to know what it felt like to run a knife through someone's heart, but somehow to bungle it, and then to heave a long sigh of relief. The impulse would have been satisfied, that was the main thing; satisfied without any awkward consequences. A lot of people, especially men, will have had this feeling. They will have encountered it in small, everyday situations. There is something that is annoying you, you dash it to the ground and then you are filled with remorse because you've broken it. That wasn't your intention.

Irma sat up. Very quietly and deliberately, speaking the words out loud, she said, 'I am a decent and honourable person. I must pay the price for what I have done.'

What she meant by this was that she would have to die. There was a little mother-of-pearl-handled revolver in her vanity case. She glanced over to where it was kept.

'What is the point of me anyway?' she asked herself. 'None. Who cares what becomes of me?' She smiled a bitter little smile. She thought of the Hungarian blacksmith to whom she still had not given the two hundred *lire*. Then she gave a start. There were voices coming from her mother's room. She knew she was not mistaken. One of them was Judith's. She opened the door to the living-room. She could hear Judith's voice quite distinctly, she was explaining something to Mrs Lietzen, something that was taking her some time to make clear. Irma looked at herself in the mirror as if to fortify herself, then opened her mother's door and went in. Judith was standing next to the bed. On seeing Irma, she instantly fell silent.

'You're back!' exclaimed Mrs Lietzen. 'Oh!—If only you knew what's been going on!'

Patiently listening to Mrs Lietzen's account was a test of all Irma's strength, but the fact of Judith's presence made it easier for her to stay silent, pressing her trembling knees together beneath the folds of her skirt. Her face gave nothing away. It could not turn any paler than the visage she had just seen staring out at her from the looking-glass. She stood quietly, pretending to pay attention to her mother's gabbling. From the hasty, garbled tale, no more than a few words stood out and made sense.

'…brooch—in Judith's trunk… She brought it to me in the dead of night… Hotel manager…detective…waiter… They have released Judith now—the waiter too…'

Irma was beginning to find it unbearable. Her nerves were in tatters, she wanted to scream. And then suddenly, her knees stopped shaking. Four words floated out of the chaotic morass and lodged themselves in her brain:

'He has been detained.'

'*He*?' she asked, feeling the sudden clutch of ice-cold fingers round her heart. 'Who?'

Her mother pronounced the syllables of the name she had somehow failed to hear the first time:

'Aurelian.'

Irma stared at her mother with an expression of supreme calm. 'Aurelian? But why?'

You must face up to it, poppet, Mrs Lietzen thought. Out loud, she said, 'The policeman who was here earlier is clinging to his theory. Which is that—which is that Aurelian stole the brooch and hid it in Judith's room. And that—that Judith, full of remorse, brought it back to me.'

'Aurelian—Aurelian stole it?'

Let's get it over with, Mrs Lietzen decided.

'Aurelian was with Judith in her room last night,' she said.

Until this point Irma had not looked at Judith. But it had been instinctive, it had never occurred to her that she was avoiding eye-contact. Now, however, it required a conscious effort not to look at Judith. Calmly and without saying a word, she left the room, crossed the living-room and returned to her own bedroom. Mrs Lietzen sighed. Irma's silence betokened so much suffering. It was completely understandable.

Irma stood at the window, staring blankly at the water and at the pink bell-tower on the further shore. She felt hollow. All she could think of was that Aurelian had been in Judith's room the night before. And that now he had been detained by the police.

I have got to get away from all this, she told herself. She stared out of the window. I want to die, she thought. Down on the quay she saw someone raise a hand. It was Nino. He was still waiting. How many people's lives have I turned upside down? she wondered. She moved away from the window. She felt unsteady on her feet. She threw herself onto the bed again.

It is a wonderful, mysterious, life-sustaining trick that psychology plays on us; the fact that at moments of extreme inner turmoil we do not focus on what has caused it, but on sundry little peripheral things, or on wider generalities. We might stare with the deepest concentration at the antics of a fly, or lose ourselves in the great question of the purpose of human existence.

I am not of my time. That was the line of thinking to which Irma's mind had recourse. To look at, she told herself, you would think I was an ultra-modern young woman, but deep down I'm exactly like my grandmother was when she was young, at the end of the last century. But it's not my fault that I'm like this. It's Mother's doing. No—that's not fair. It isn't Mother's fault. It's Daddy's money, that's what's done it. Darling Daddy...' She fell into a deep torpor. It is a blessing from Heaven, in a way, the ability to anaesthetise oneself, quite naturally, without the aid of any drug. A complete numbing of the senses just comes of its own accord. Irma lay with her eyes wide open, staring sightlessly into space, her mind a perfect blank.

She lay like that until gradually, imperceptibly, she became aware of a voice. Someone was talking to her. With difficulty, she turned her face in its direction. Her father was standing by her bedside.

Suddenly she was wide awake, as if she had just that minute been born.

'Daddy!' she cried. A vision of the silver seaplane flashed into her mind, a memory of the day her father had suddenly and irretrievably vanished into thin air.

Her father was saying something to her but she did not hear him because suddenly it was she who wanted to do the talking, all at once, feverishly, in a great flood of words. She felt like a sick patient who has no time for anyone or anything and who only begins to behave like a normal human being when at last—at last!—the doctor arrives.

'Daddy, it was me! *I* did it! I—I took it out of Mother's evening bag. I—I sneaked it into Judith's room. I hid it in her trunk. Daddy, oh Daddy, I'll kill myself if anything happens to him because of this!'

With a sudden jerk, like a fish drowning on a river bank, she pulled herself upright and then turned flat on her face. In a voice that was stifled by the pillow, she cried,

'You've got to help me, Daddy! *I* did it! And now—now someone else is in trouble.'

Mr Lietzen stared at her, all the colour drained from his face.

'Have you gone mad?'

'It was me, *me*!' came the voice from the pillow. '*I* did it, because I wanted Judith to... Because he loves her... I wanted to kill her...'

Then she heard her mother's voice. She lifted her head and looked up. She had the same ghoulish look that terrified horses get, when all you can see is the whites of their eyes. Staring straight at her mother, she cried, 'It was me, I swear!'

Mr Lietzen just stood there in utter consternation. He stroked his daughter's thick fair hair. He tried to make his voice sound calm and reassuring.

'There, there, my dear, you're in love. That's what the trouble is. It's making you want to sacrifice yourself for—for the sake of the man you adore. But you mustn't take on so. You must try and clam down.'

'No, Daddy, I swear it was me who did it! I'll swear it by anything you like. I'll swear on your life, on Mother's life...' A hideous kind of panic began to fill her. They'll never believe me, she thought. They'll never believe I'm telling the truth...

Salvation came from the quarter she was least expecting. Mrs Lietzen burst into tears and said, on a stifled sob,

'Every word she says is true. I can vouch for it, Stephen.

234

She's telling the truth.'

'She's in love,' Mr Lietzen insisted, in the tone of voice one might use when saying, 'She doesn't know what she's saying,' or 'She's lost her mind.'

'Yes, she's in love,' said Mrs Lietzen. 'And that's precisely the reason why I believe her. And you must believe her too.'

Mr Lietzen, who was beginning to find himself in unfamiliar psychological territory, began to pace nervously up and down. He would never have done such a thing in Lionel Rothschild's office. In an office environment he knew how to retain full mastery of himself. Now, though, faced with these two women, he felt like a gormless schoolboy. Much later, looking back on it all, he expressed it as follows: 'I felt exactly like a right foot in a left shoe.'

Finally, he was forced to admit defeat. He looked at the bed, where his poor, distraught daughter was lying, flat on her back again, her eyes vacant and staring.

'It's all right, my dear,' he said. 'We'll sort it all out. You'd better come with me to the police station.'

In an instant, Irma had sprung to her feet. The little dark blue hat was already on her head. And the eyes that she turned on her father were filled with fervent devotion.

They took the shortest route to the San Lorenzo police station, going by water, along the canals. Irma was wide awake again, alert to everything, completely in possession of herself and aware of her surroundings. Her dominant emotion was impatience at how slowly their boat was progressing. In the narrowest canals it was only allowed to go at half speed. But at least they were moving. They were on their way. Only a few more minutes and justice would be done. And she would be able to live again. Once again she was aware of that strange, almost tangible sense of happiness. She was leaving all her pain behind. In a kind of trance, her heart singing, she looked about her at the little world they were so cautiously traversing. How different the narrow slit of the canal felt today, hemmed in by bright red walls, from the way it had been on that fateful night when she and Judith had got lost in the Middle Ages. Coming towards them in the opposite direction were a couple of goods barges, painted bright blue. One of them was laden to the gunwales with brand new wooden crates, the other bulged with sacks of flour. And then came another, packed with a million soda siphons—petrol cans—mountains of lettuces. The barges were propelled along by laughing young men, stripped to the waist, shouting at the top of their voices. This was the real-life Venice of the early morning, a Venice where everyone is hard at work. A Venice that does not give two hoots for the opinion of the city's dinner-jacketed international hotel clientèle. And how colourful it all was! Irma looked down at the churning blue water as it lapped and sucked at lime green, algae-encrusted marble pediments. And then she cast her gaze upward, at the sun, which shone high above them, casting the benison of its kindly rays into their tiny, narrow slit, richly gilding successive sections of crumbling red-brick wall. The air was clamorous with the sounds of morning: from one window, the noise of a saw rasped its way out into the canal; from another came the workshop din of clanging hammers; from yet another a voice was heard, raised in song. And the myriad bird cages suspended from the upper-storey windows filled the air with a tremulous warbling. It filled each and every canal with the kind of twittering that one never hears in an actual forest. It is an intensity of sound such as one only hears in pet shops. And up at the very highest level, on the rooftops, among the flowerpots of the little *altana* balconies, it was as if the houses had put out bunting. The rooftops flapped with drying laundry, the domestic poetry of the south, as the morning sun made sport with children's blouses, pink pillow slips and pairs of cotton trousers pegged upside down. 'Dell'Osmarin' announced the sign on a corner, followed by a laughing face, Chaplin, on a poster stuck to a blood-red *palazzo* condemned to the whims of the water. From behind a brick wall, a tiny leafy garden spilled out over the canal. And on the next corner, beside a tabernacle of the Virgin with its vase of flowers and its flickering lamp, festooned with tinsel offerings, was a white advertising hoarding with a single printed word: 'PILSEN'. And life, life was being lived everywhere, noisily, greedily...

'San Lorenzo!' said the boat driver, as the engine fell silent.

Irma and her father climbed the steps onto the quay, then went through the portals of the police station, emblazoned with the city's shield and coat of arms. In the low-ceilinged entrance hall, with its red flagstones and squat, red marble columns, Mr Lietzen stopped and gave a wry little smile.

'In the Venice of the olden days,' he said, 'a good-for-nothing like you would have been locked up in an iron cage just big enough for you to crouch in, and then hoisted up on a great pole and suspended from the top of the Campanile. For two days and two nights, without food or water.'

His daughter, infused with a burgeoning new lease of life, was making her way towards the stairs.

'And in the Venice of today?' she called over her shoulder.

'Oh, just the same as everywhere else in the world. And just as it always will be, for as long as the world keeps turning. Your silly old ass of a father will stump up a wad of cash.'

At the top of the stairs on the first floor, a heavy door fell shut behind them. It stayed shut for a long, long time.

And then at last they came out, and slowly made their way down the stairs again.

'Is everything all right now?'

Irma said nothing. She just nodded, rapidly and repeatedly. Yes, yes, yes. Slowly the colour was coming back into her cheeks.

When they reached the quayside, her father began to make his way towards their boat.

'Not yet,' she said. 'Let's wait.'

'What for?'

'I want to see him. I—I want to be sure that he's been released.'

They waited for a few minutes. Then they saw Aurelian, hurriedly leaving the building. Mr Lietzen went over to him.

'My boy,' he said, 'a sixty-year-old, humiliated man humbly begs for your forgiveness.' He held out his hand.

'Sir...'

Aurelian took off his hat and bowed. He took Mr Lietzen's proffered hand and Mr Lietzen grasped it between both his own, in a tight sandwich. Irma was staring at Aurelian as if he had been the one to save *her* life rather than the other way round. As if... But let us not dwell on such things. Aurelian did not look at Irma. Quietly, awkwardly, he said,

'Would you excuse me? I've got someone waiting...'

The stiff little bow he gave was directed ever so slightly in Irma's direction too. And then he began to hurry along the wide quayside, back towards the centre of town. He was literally running, and Irma knew exactly why, and exactly where he was hurrying, and to whom. And it no longer hurt.

Back at the hotel, Mr Lietzen went with the manager into his office. Then the door opened and the manager ushered him out, bowing with his customary obsequious, fugitive smirk. His lips snapped back, but this time only into semi-expressionlessness. A trace of the smirk remained, a clear sign that the hotel's reputation was safe; that the fullest discretion had been promised and was assured. Mr Lietzen was good at that kind of thing.

Mrs Lietzen knew only too well the direction in which her husband's talents lay. Back in their hotel room, she asked dismally, 'How much did you give him?'

Mr Lietzen dropped his eyes, like a child who has been caught red-handed.

Judith was no longer with them. She was long gone, together with her travelling trunk. 'In case there is anything else I can do for you', she had left her address: Pensione Corti.

The print tablecloth, the little entranceway, the concierge, the dented matchbox holder. Judith had gone home. She was in her true element. But…

But Mr Lietzen was uneasy. He thought he should have offered her rather a lot of money.

'Oh, let it go,' said his wife, who was seated at her dressing table, peering at herself in the silver mirror.

'That's certainly what *we* must do, at any rate,' said Mr Lietzen. 'Go, I mean. Get away from here. As soon as we possibly can.'

'Where to?' came Mrs Lietzen's voice, speaking from within the mirror's silver frame.

'Switzerland?' Mr Lietzen suggested, raising his voice for the benefit of Irma, who was lying on her mother's unmade bed, her eyes closed.

Irma shook her head. 'No.'

'A cruise?' said her father, upping his bid. 'Norway, the fjords? Spitzbergen?'

'No,' said Irma again, quietly.

'Where, then?'

Irma's voice had sunk to a barely audible whisper. 'I want to go home.'

Mr Lietzen said nothing. And then the voice came again, even quieter than ever.

'Home to the Danube.'

From behind her closed lids, now moist with welling tears, she could see the great expanse of water stretching beyond Tahi. The peaceful noonday calm; geese paddling across to the island; a great big black ungainly barge floating slowly downstream, with its bright white, tin-roofed doghouse at one end, the living quarters of the crew, a little box garden in front of it, with runner beans trained on poles and wire. And at Tótfalu[22], a white boat at the jetty, whistling cheerfully before it set off, gently whipping up the water at its bow, then gradually chugging out of sight as it glided towards Budapest. Far away in the distance, in the sweet suspension of the summer heat, the sound of it receding downstream was like the very heartbeat of the river itself, soft and rhythmic and even…

'I'll have the car made ready today.'

'No—oh no! It will take too long if we go by car. I want to be there now!'

'Very well, my dear, we'll take the train.'

The following day, after lunch, a large motor boat piled high with luggage, all of it pockmarked with hotel stickers, could be seen making its way towards the Grand Canal, bound for the railway station. Seated on one side, in her red hat, was Mrs Lietzen, clutching her enormous jewellery box, her crocodile handbag and the vanity case from Paris which contained her gold cosmetic set. Opposite her was Mr Lietzen, with his beautiful, sick, convalescent daughter collapsed across one shoulder, her sad blonde head lost in a semi-slumber. The boat was passing the Piazzetta, from where there was an excellent view of St Mark's Basilica.

'Look, St Mark's!' said Mr Lietzen, craning his neck as it went past. 'Don't you want to say goodbye to it?'

He could feel the blonde head shaking 'no' on his shoulder. The boat slowed down. It had reached the point where there were *palazzi* on both sides and where it was no longer permissible to travel at speed. No one said a word but every now and then, when they went past a particularly notable building, Mrs Lietzen let out a sigh. Irma kept her head buried in her father's shoulder, her eyes closed. She was spent, exhausted, broken. She did not want to catch even a single last glimpse of the marble marvel she was leaving behind. Mr Lietzen took out his watch, taking care not to move his shoulder too much under Irma's head. Irma heard him say to her mother,

'We still have a great deal of time. You always make me

leave so long before we really need to, nagging on at me about missing the train. It's like this every single time. How many times have I told myself that…'

Without stirring or opening its eyes, the blonde head that lay pressed against his shoulder suddenly spoke. 'In that case I've got a request, Daddy.'

'What's that, my dear?'

'I'd like to stop at a certain church. Just for a minute…'

'By all means, dearest,' said Lietzen.

The red hat nodded its assent. It was a reasonable request, a mother could understand it.

Mr Lietzen spoke to the driver.

'Stop at the next church.'

The blonde head spoke again, louder than before. 'At the Frari. It's on the way. Santa Maria Gloriosa dei Frari…'

'Very well, my dear, whatever you say. To the Frari, please, and stop there for a minute.'

They disembarked on the edge of the wide square in front of the enormous red-brick church. Mr Lietzen took his daughter's arm and guided her up the steps. They went in through the side door. An unctuous old man was sitting at a table. With an apologetic expression he looked up at Mr Lietzen and mumbled, '*Tre lire*.'

Three people, three *lire*. Two francs for the moon. One franc for Jupiter. Three *lire* for the Frari.

The church was full of visitors, idly wandering about and marvelling at their surroundings. In a hushed whisper, a man proffered his services as a guide.

'No need,' said Mr Lietzen.

'We're going to see the Bellini *Madonna*,' said Irma. 'It's in the sacristy.'

Mr Lietzen turned to the spurned guide. 'The sacristy?'

'Over there.' The man pointed.

Irma hurried off in the direction of his finger. Behind her, she heard her mother whispering to her father.

'And just for telling you "Over there," you give the fellow money?'

'Of course.'

The sombre sacristy was empty. It was a large room, large enough to be a whole church in its own right. To one side, a door stood open on a vista of sun-soaked lawn. At the far end, glimmering in the semi-gloom, was the great altar triptych. The light from the side windows was screened by heavy yellow curtains. Mrs Lietzen pointed. Being in a church, her practical side had come to the fore.

'It's so that the sunlight doesn't damage the precious altarpiece.'

The precious altarpiece gleamed in the golden half-light, giving off an unassuming glow from the confines of its sturdy gilded frame. In the centre sat the *Madonna Gloriosa*, with the *Bambino* standing on her knee. Wordlessly the Lietzens stood in front of it. Then Irma tiptoed forwards, moving closer to the altar rail.

'I'd like to be alone for a little bit if you don't mind,' she said, then knelt down in front of the painting.

Mr Lietzen obediently wandered off, and after hesitating a little, Mrs Lietzen did the same. They came to a standstill at the back of the room, staring in silence for what seemed like a long time. They assumed that Irma was praying but there was not much time left. The motorboat was waiting outside with the luggage.

Irma stared intently at the altarpiece but it was not the Madonna that held her attention. Her eyes were fixed on the bottom right-hand corner, anxiously seeking something among the shadows. At last her features broke into a smile. There it was. The chubby little infant angel, the angel musician. Even his wings were pudgy. He stood with one stout little leg raised up on a step, his round cheeks puffed out as he blew into his flute. Irma felt suddenly suffused with a feeling of delicious warmth. For several long minutes she just stared, smiling a painful, shy little half-smile.

'So it's you,' she said. 'So *you're* the Venetian angel.'

Patiently, in the gathering gloom, her parents waited.

Notes

1. (p. 17) Szentendre is a small town on the Danube, 20km north of Budapest.

2. (p. 18) Tahifalu, now Tahitótfalu, on an arm of the Danube some 30km north of Budapest. Opposite it, on Szentendre Island, which divides the Danube in two at this point, is Tótfalu. Many well-to-do families, as well as artists and writers, had summer houses here.

3. (p. 20) György Dózsa, a Transylvanian, was the leader of a peasant uprising in 1514. He was allegedly put to death by being seated on a red-hot throne and crowned with a red-hot crown.

4. (p. 33) Nándor Horváth, grocer, purveyor of compotes, conserves and fruit to the royal and imperial court of Austria-Hungary.

5. (p. 37) István Tisza was Prime Minister of Hungary from 1913. Against his will took Hungary into the First World War. He was assassinated in 1918, during the revolution that swept a Hungarian People's Republic to power.

6. (p. 37) Mihály Munkácsy (1844–1900) was the most celebrated Hungarian painter of his day.

7. (p. 38) Parád mineral water, known for its high sulphur content, comes from the Mátra hills in north Hungary.

8. (p. 58) Winnaretta Singer (1865–1943), American heiress to the eponymous sewing-machine fortune, bought Palazzo Contarini dal Zaffo on the Grand Canal for her husband, Prince Edmond de Polignac, in 1900. She was a great patron of music. The *palazzo* still contains pianos played by Poulenc and Fauré.

9. (p. 59) Andrew III died in 1301, just a few months after his Venetian mother. Sources suggest that both were the victims of poisoning.

10. (p. 62) 'Would you like to look round the shop?' 'No, thank

you.' 'It's all genuine Bohemian glass.'

11. (p. 62) Tokaj is Hungary's premier wine region, producing a famous dessert wine.

12. (p. 68) 'God give you [a good day]' and 'Good day!'

13. (p. 76) Pitigrilli, pseudonym of the novelist and journalist Dino Segre (1893–1975). His most famous novel was placed on the prohibition list by the Catholic Church because of the frank way it deals with the topics of sex and drugs.

14. (p. 78) Vác, a town on the main arm of the Danube, on the other side of Szentendre Island from Tahi (Tahitótfalu; *see Note 1*). It is a scenic stretch of the river, just at the point where the Danube begins to bend.

15. (p. 99) *Occasione*. Denoting goods offered at reduced prices.

16. (p. 109) Abbazia is the old Austro-Hungarian name for Opatija, in present-day Croatia.

17. (p. 110) Péter Pázmány (1570–1637), Jesuit cleric, a prominent figure of the Counter-Reformation in Hungary.

18. (p. 145) Fiume, a city on the Adriatic coast. When this novel was written, it was part of the Kingdom of Italy. Today it is in Croatia and is called Rijeka.

19. (p. 186) The actress Eleonora Duse (1858–1924) and the writer and war hero Gabriele d'Annunzio (1863–1938) lived in the Casina delle Rose on the Grand Canal during the time of their love affair in 1895. Palazzo Contarini-Fasan, futher east along the Grand Canal on the same side, is a narrow 15th-century *palazzo* that was once a tower from where a chain was slung across the Canal to close it. Its history as the home of Desdemona is legendary.

20. (p. 187) The Hortobágy is an area of the Hungarian Great Plain, known for its cattle tended by mounted herdsmen.

21. (p. 210) The *pengő* was the currency of Hungary from 1927–46.

22. (p. 241) Tótfalu: see Note 1.